THE UNDERTAKER:
DESTINED TO DIE

The Undertaker series by George G. Gilman,
available from New English Library:

THE UNDERTAKER 1: BLACK AS DEATH
THE UNDERTAKER 2: DESTINED TO DIE

THE UNDERTAKER: DESTINED TO DIE

George G. Gilman

NEW ENGLISH LIBRARY/TIMES MIRROR

For:
Ed Bruce – they just have to let cowboys in, don't they?

A New English Library Original Publication, 1981

First NEL Paperback Edition July 1981

NEL Books are published by
New English Library Limited,
Barnard's Inn, Holborn,
London EC1N 2JR.

Made and printed in Great Britain by
Hunt Barnard Printing Ltd,
Aylesbury, Bucks.

0 450 05195 1

CHAPTER ONE

IT was an hour after sun up, but the sun could not be seen through the heavy cloud layer that was spread across the sky above the Mohave Mountains, when Barnaby Gold reined in his black gelding and looked down at the small homestead on the east bank of the Colorado River.

But it was as hot as the threshold of hell. Damper, though, for the high humidity felt like a blanket steeped in water pressing against his skin. And his face was beaded with moisture, the sweat standing out on his flesh like raindrops which had fallen invisibly from the clouds.

It was the good-looking face of a young man in his mid-twenties. Lean, like his six foot tall frame: but whereas there was little outward sign of the physical strength commanded by his lanky body and rather gangling limbs, the face revealed an undoubted strength of character. This showed most prominently in the green eyes, which surveyed the world with confidence – as if whatever remained to be seen of it could hold no surprises. Also in the set of the mouth, which in repose was firm: and looked more ready to smile than to scowl. But either would require an effort.

The forehead, the nose, the bone structure of the cheeks and jaws, and the ears were all regular in form and the skin was evenly tanned and unblemished. His hair was blond in colour and neatly trimmed.

He was dressed entirely in black.

A hat that was something between a Stetson and a Derby, a frock coat worn open to show a shirt buttoned to the throat, pants which had once been part of a suit and riding boots.

With the exception of the hat, which he had confiscated from a dead man, his clothing had once been part of his professional garb. But he was no longer an undertaker of Fairfax, Arizona Territory. Neither was he what might be suggested by the gunbelt fastened around his waist. A belt which was hung on the right with a conventional holster tied down to the thigh and holding a wood-butted Colt .45 Peacemaker. With, fitted to the right by a stud in a slot, another Peacemaker, eagle-butted in mother-of-pearl. Even though two powder-burned holes in the area of the frock coat's left pocket showed that the wearer had made use of the swivel-rigged gun.

Down at the homestead beside the river, a man emerged from a rear door of the single storey house, strode across the yard and entered a barn. A young man from the way he walked. And one with urgent business elsewhere, judging by the speed with which he saddled a horse and galloped away: heading north-east along a trail that followed the course of the shallow, forty foot wide river.

Barnaby Gold watched the rider out of sight into some timber and when he returned his expressionless eyes to the house he saw black woodsmoke beginning to wisp from the chimney. Then he took the time to light a long, thin cheroot before clucking his horse forward: to ride down a long, gentle incline which was dusty and rocky, toward the well-watered and carefully tended fields of growing crops behind the house and barn.

The Denver saddle in which he sat creaked a little as he rode but the twin bags, the canteens and the bedroll tied on behind, remained steady where they were fastened. Just the double barrel, hammerless Murcott shotgun – hung by a hook to the right front rigging ring – moved slightly with the motion of the horse.

Down on the bottom land at the foot of the slope, he veered his mount to the right, then the left. To ride around the unfenced property to the east and north of the house and barn: so as not to trample the plots of wheat, barley and sugarbeet.

He could smell frying bacon in the woodsmoke now. And a citrus aroma from the lemon grove to the south of the house. Then heard a woman singing – la-la-laing some of the lyrics she had forgotten – as he turned on to the trail that dead-ended on an area some forty feet wide between the stooped front of the house and the sluggishly flowing, mud-coloured water of the Colorado. She sounded like a very young woman. And curtailed the song with the abruptness of alarm when Barnaby Gold reined in his horse and called: 'Good morning.'

Her face showed at an uncurtained window two to the right of the closed door. Wearing an expression that was a match for the way in which she had finished the song. Very young – not even a woman. A girl of no more than thirteen.

Gold remained in the saddle, as motionless as his mount, ten feet away from the front of the house and facing it. Eyeing her expectantly. But the girl did not call out to her parents: just stared through the window at him with curiosity gradually displacing fear on her immature features.

'Appreciate it if your folks have some of that hot breakfast to spare, little lady.'

She nodded and turned from the window.

Gold swung down from the saddle, led his horse forward and hitched the reins to a post that supported the stoop roof.

Two bolts were slid and a chain rattled before the door folded open on silent hinges. And the girl stepped over the threshold. She was about five feet five inches tall and more than slim, the all-engulfing white cotton nightgown she wore seeming to touch her only at the shoulders and wrists. She had very long, dark red hair, untidy from sleeping, that reached almost to her waist after framing her oval-shaped, angular-featured face. Her eyes were large, the pupils a soft brown colour. Freckles were scattered to either side of her snub nose. Her top teeth were a little too large and protruded slightly. 'My folks ain't here right now, mister. But you're welcome to have some breakfast. On one condition.'

She was not native to this Arizona–California border area, her strong accent placing her origins in Kentucky or Tennessee.

'What's that?'

'My name is Joanne. Joanne Engel. I don't like to be called little lady or stuff like that.'

'Okay.'

'What's your name, mister?'

'Barnaby Gold.'

'I call my parents by their first names.'

'Okay, just Barnaby.'

She turned to lead the way into the house. And by accident or design, her arms pressed the fabric of the nightgown to her sides. Which had the effect of drawing the thin cotton taut over the low, twin contours of her adolescent breasts.

Gold took off his hat and dragged a coat sleeve across his sweat-tacky forehead as he followed her inside. He left the door open: struck a match on the frame to relight the cheroot which had gone out since he removed it from his lips to call the greeting.

'You make yourself at home now,' the girl offered, 'while I put some more bacon in the pan. Coffee'll be ready in next to no time.'

There was definitely an exaggerated sway to her hips under the capacious nightgown as she walked across the parlour and through an open doorway.

Gold clicked his tongue against the roof of his mouth and went to sit down in one of two matching padded armchairs that flanked a stone fireplace. The furniture in the wooden walled room was plain, worn and comfortable. Some dozen or so books on a shelf to the right of the fireplace and a piano angled across a corner near the window were the only trimmings. There were no pictures on the white painted walls nor any rugs on the boarded floor.

'You think it's gonna rain, Barnaby?'

'I don't know,' he answered the question called from the kitchen.

'It certainly looks so from the sky. Not that it makes much difference to us. Having the river and all. But some rain would be nice. Cool things down some, wouldn't you say?'

She was trying to sound older than her years, but there was a note of strain in her voice. Like she was a bad actress playing a part unsuited to her.

'Guess so.'

'You ain't much of a talker, are you?'

'Not much.'

She began to sing again. The same song as before. A lyric about mountains and rivers and a man who would not return. The bacon sizzled in appetising but monotonous accompaniment. Then she brought in a tin mug of coffee.

'Thanks.'

'You're surely welcome. I'll just go put some clothes on and by then it'll be ready to eat.'

'Okay.'

She swayed toward a door on the other side of the room. Left it open behind her. Beyond was a short hallway with a door to either side. Her bedroom was at the rear of the house. She left its door open, too. Began to hum the same tune while water was poured into a basin. Then came splashing sounds.

Barnaby Gold smoked his cheroot and took small sips of the scalding, very strong coffee. Decided it was pointless to try to keep from his mind a vivid image of the girl's slender naked body run with water just two open doors and maybe twenty feet away from him. The thoughts caused a stirring of lust at his crotch, but the sweat which oozed from his pores continued to be due entirely to the un-Arizonalike humidity of the morning. Joanne Engel was just a child.

And when she emerged from her bedroom, she looked almost every inch what she was. Her hair was brushed and tied at the nape of her neck in two ponytails and she wore a pink and white gingham dress: short sleeved, high at the neck and with a hem that reached to just below her knees. White socks covered her legs and on her feet was a pair of brass-buckled black leather shoes. The swells of her embryonic breasts and the curves of her hips below the narrow waist were emphasised by the close fit of the dress. A child aware of approaching womanhood, obviously proud of her blossoming and eager for full bloom.

'There, that's better,' she said with a bright smile. 'Before, I was in no fit state to receive a gentleman caller.'

Gold showed a personable smile – an expression which, throughout his life, had given countless strangers pause for thought about their first impression of him. As it did on this occasion, while the girl was taking the things from a bureau to set two places at a table.

'And that's better, too. Why, when I first looked out at you, I had the fright of my life, Barnaby. Sitting there on that black horse, and you dressed all in black the way you are. And not smiling. You looked like . . . well, I don't know what. But not friendly, that's for sure.'

He rose from the chair and set his empty mug on the mantelshelf that was bare of ornaments.

'Didn't mean to scare you. Be okay if I water my horse?'

'Certainly. There's a trough in the barn. And leave him in there if you've a mind. In case it rains. Not too long now.'

He went out and unhitched the reins from the post. Overhead, the cloud cover was thinning and the orb of the sun could be seen, whitish, above the ridges of the Mohave Mountains. Gold led the gelding across the front of the house, along the side and on to the yard out back. Another horse in the barn snorted when he pushed open the door and led the gelding inside.

In fact, there were two horses in the barn. A grey and a chestnut. Both mares, occupying the only stalls. There was a trough at the rear, beside a stack of half a dozen hay bales and some sacks of oats. Gold allowed his mount to drink then hitched him to the offside front wheel of a cut-under wagon, neatly parked against a side wall.

Then, as he straightened up from slackening the saddle cinch, he did a double-take over the rump of the horse at something he had glimpsed from a more acute angle beneath the animal's belly. And saw he was not mistaken. That, protruding from near the edge of an elongated patch of newly dug earth . . . there was a man's finger.

CHAPTER TWO

SINCE, at the age of twelve, he had been apprenticed to his father's undertaking business in New York City, Barnaby Gold experienced no sense of horror as – using a shovel taken from a rack of tools on the barn wall – he scraped aside some loose dirt from around the finger. To expose a work-gnarled hand. And enough of a shirt-sleeved arm so that he was able to get down on his haunches, take a double-handed grip on the dead flesh and haul the corpse partway out of the shallow grave.

Just one arm and shoulder, the head and upper right quarter of the torso.

'Barnaby! I'm putting the food on the table now!'

She sounded like a mother summoning her reluctant offspring to leave a favourite game and come eat. Gold thought it likely that it was the hand of her own mother which was hooked over the shirt collar of the man partially dragged from the double grave. For he was certainly her father – despite the crumbs of dirt clinging to the dead flesh, the family resemblance between the thirty-some-year-old man and the girl was obvious.

'You hear me, Barnaby?'

'I hear you.'

He inched the man out of the dirt some more. Just

enough to see the bullet hole, encircled by crusted blood, in his chest, left of centre.

The woman had a slighter build than the man and it was much easier to bring her far enough out of the ground to see that she had been killed in the same way. Her hair was the same colour as that of Joanne and her upper teeth also protruded slightly. In death, her eyes were closed. Her face was so contorted by agony or anguish, it was difficult to tell if she had been a pretty woman. The man had died with his eyes open, expressing a shock less intense than the woman had left. His face was rough-hewn, not quite ugly.

Barnaby Gold straightened up and brushed his hands clean of dirt, rather than to free them of the touch of limp, cold, newly dead flesh. Then went out of the barn, blinking in the brightness of a sun which had punched a hole in the clouds. He re-entered the house through the rear door from which the young man in a hurry had emerged earlier.

It gave on to a kitchen hot with stove heat and redolent with the aromas of recently fried bacon and brewed coffee.

'And about time, too. Ain't nothing worse than bacon when the grease starts to cool.'

She was seated at one side of the table, already started on the breakfast of bacon, beans and grits. A plate with an equal amount of food was in front of the empty chair. Along with a mug of fresh coffee. The detached attitude of Barnaby Gold, which hardly ever altered – except when he smiled – gave Joanne Engel no premonition of his discovery.

'You want to tell me about your folks?'

He bypassed the table to go to the fireplace: tossed the stub of the cheroot into the empty grate.

'Virgil and Mary-Ann?' she responded conversationally. 'Them and me, we come from the Great Smokey Mountains in Tennessee. Like a lot of the folks hereabouts. Moved out to this neck of the woods . . .'

She allowed the sentence to hang in the hot air, bright with sunlight streaming in through the east-facing window. And turned on her chair to look at him – standing before the fireplace. Her head was cocked to one side and there seemed to be genuine puzzlement in her soft brown eyes.

'You found them?'

'Right.'

She began to cry. Abruptly, tears filled her big eyes and spilled down her freckled cheeks. For long moments there was no sound from her. Then she dropped her fork to the floor, covered her face with her hands and vented a wail.

'Shut up.'

She curtailed the sound but kept her face covered. 'What?'

'It's as fake as your grown-up act.'

She let her hands fall into her lap. 'Shit, they were my parents!'

'Been dead for most of the night. You'd be through weeping about that, if you felt bad about it. Don't even think you're sorry you killed them. You or the guy I saw riding out on the trail awhile back.'

She used the backs of her hands to rub the salty moisture from her eyes. And stood up violently, so that her chair fell over backwards.

'Jesse! Jesse Gershel. You saw him leave here, Barnaby?'

'If that's who he was.'

'I'm not going to protect him! Why should I? He's nothing to me! Just a hillbilly rube! He took me in just because he was the only man around here to show any interest in me! What a fool I've been!'

She took two steps toward Gold, but the lack of emotion in his green eyes extended no invitation to come closer. Then he moved. Swinging to go around her to the table. Where he sat down and began to eat the breakfast she had prepared.

'You just going to leave it there?' she asked hoarsely: and her surprise was definitely genuine.

'How old are you, Joanne?'

'I'm . . . ' She was going to lie, but decided against it. 'Shit, I'm twelve, going on near thirteen.'

He swallowed some beans and clicked his tongue against the roof of his mouth.

'Just that? Tell me why?' A fresh spell of weeping was in the offing. Not the histrionic variety.

Gold nodded. 'Right. You're just a kid, older in mind than body. There was a chance you were in a state of shock after whatever happened that got your parents killed. But that's not the way it is. So I'll just eat and be on my way. None of this is any of my business. And kid you may be, but I figure you're in control of the situation.'

'I'm not, I'm not! I need help! I was gonna tell you everything that happened! But I just couldn't think how to do it! So I just put on that act of being calm and all . . . while I was thinking!'

'You did it real well.'

She set her chair upright and dropped on to it as violently as she had left the table. And stared intently across at him.

'Please, Barnaby! Jesse came by last night. While my folks was over at a neighbour's place. He sweet-talked me into going with him.' She shook her head, the ponytails swinging. 'Shit, I ain't saying I wasn't ready to be sweet-talked that way. I ain't saying I tried to fight him off or nothing. And I ain't saying I didn't enjoy it and all.'

Gold looked up from his plate and was certain there was a tacit suggestion in her eyes that she was willing to demonstrate her brand of enjoyment between the sheets.

'You're not exciting me, Joanne,' he lied.

She scowled, but not for long. 'We fell asleep, Barnaby. Didn't hear Virgil and Mary-Ann drive back to the house. They found us together in my bed. Naked as when we were born. Virgil, he went crazy. And I'm sure as sure he would've killed Jesse if Jesse hadn't got his gun first. Mary-Ann, she just kept on screaming and screaming. No different after Virgil was dead than when she'd first seen me and Jesse in the bed. Jesse, he just told her to stop. And when she wouldn't, he shot her, too. I never touched no gun, Barnaby. I swear it.'

Gold rattled his fork down on his empty plate. And finished the last of the fresh mug of coffee.

'I believe you,' he said as he stood up and pushed his chair back.

She shook her head again. 'And I never helped him to bury the bodies out to the barn, neither. Jesse, he said it had to be done. That afterwards he'd ride home and say he'd been out drinking in Bacall. I was to wait until this morning. Then go see Will and Martha – his parents. Say how worried I was that my folks hadn't got back yet from visiting the Wolfes up at Bent River Crossing.'

Gold had taken a cheroot from the tin box he carried in an inside pocket of his frock coat. Now he struck a match on the butt of the Peacemaker in the holster and lit the tobacco. He let the dead match fall on to the greasy plate.

She stood up, hands gripping the edge of the table: her immature breasts heaving with powerful emotion.

'I don't want to go along with all that, Barnaby! Last night, when he told it to me, I agreed. But I don't now. Even before you found Virgil and Mary-Ann. I knew folks wouldn't go along with the idea that they was taken by Injuns or fell into the river and got swept away.'

Gold clicked his tongue and nodded. 'That's right, Joanne. Especially since the wagon and team are safe in the barn.'

'Aw, shit!'

He turned from the table. 'Bye-bye, kid.'

'I told you I didn't like that kid stuff and little lady crap!' she shrieked, suddenly a child with a temper tantrum because she had not been given what she wanted.

'I was wrong first off,' he said from the doorway that gave on to the kitchen. 'With a mouth like you have, you're not any kind of lady.'

'But I'm a woman!' she hurled back. 'Last night Jesse made me one of those!'

She whirled and ran into a bedroom. Not her own. She left the door open and Gold heard a ripping of fabric. A gasp. Then the unmistakable metallic sounds of a gun being cocked.

He started across the parlour.

She came out of her parents' bedroom, her dress torn from the neckline to the start of her shallow cleavage. Her right hand fisted around the butt of a big Army Model Starr .44 revolver.

She pulled up short as he came toward her. And squeezed the trigger. The crack of the gun sounded very loud in the confines of the parlour. The gun bucked in her hand and the exploded bullet buried itself in the wall.

A gasp of shock vented from her mouth and she struggled to thumb back the hammer again.

Gold snatched the smoking gun from her hand and hurled it into the grate of the fireplace. Gripped her shoulder with his left hand and made to bring back his right to slap her across the face.

She cowered away from him, her features showing an expression of childish terror.

He squeezed his eyes tight shut, then pushed her away from him. She slammed to a halt against the wall.

'Go on, mark me up some more.'

When he opened his eyes, her mouthline was set in a sinister smile.

'He made me a woman! And I'm not yet thirteen, mister!' She rasped the words through her bared teeth. There was a challenge implicit in her stance.

'Finish it, Joanne.'

'It's well known hereabouts that me and Jesse have been walking out. But him being twenty years old and me being what I am, well folks just wouldn't easily believe what happened. But if I was to tell them some passing stranger dressed all in black and wearing two guns on his belt came by and had his way with me – killed my folks and all like that . . . Well, Barnaby, I reckon they'd believe that easy enough. And even if I haven't killed you, you wouldn't get out of this neighbourhood alive.'

'Just what is my breakfast going to cost me, Joanne?'

The challenge, the anger and the slyness drained out of her face and attitude. And she became the pathetic, apologetic young girl: as she modestly clutched the two sides of the torn dress together.

'I'm sorry I tried to kill you, Barnaby. Take me over to the Gershel place. With you there, to tell how you found the bodies and all, I'll be able to say what really happened. Honest I will. The whole truth, just like I told it to you. And it won't matter that Jesse'll be there with his folks not ready to believe he'd do such a terrible thing.'

Her big brown eyes implored his agreement.

He sucked in lungsful of smoke and let it out in a long stream. 'Okay.'

'Oh, thank you, thank you.'

She started toward him.

He held up a hand. 'First change into a different dress.'

'I'll be forever grateful,' she said shrilly as she swung to go toward her bedroom.

Gold clicked his tongue. Muttered: 'For me, kid.'

CHAPTER THREE

AFTER Barnaby Gold Senior died from a heart seizure in the carpentry workshop behind the funeral parlour in Fairfax, his son simply wanted to bury the deceased, sell the business and fulfil a long-nurtured ambition to go to Europe.

But a series of events which had its beginning on the day of the elder Gold's funeral had interfered with this clear-cut plan.* He was still intent upon reaching a seaport from which he could board a ship to Europe, but first there was unfinished business that needed to be attended to.

He had to kill some men who were out to kill him.

Which gave him a double reason for submitting to the precocious Joanne Engel's blackmail. Primarily, it was that he did not want to have to contend with a bunch of trigger happy hillbilly farmers tracking him when he was already the target for the professional gunslingers hired by the Channons of west Texas. But allied to this was the fact that by taking the girl to her neighbours, he would establish his presence in this Arizona–California border land. And thus give the Channons' manhunters a fresh lead to their quarry after they had allowed his trail to go cold.

* *See* The Undertaker 1: Black as Death.

So this was why Barnaby Gold Junior rode with Joanne Engel aboard the heavy cut-under wagon up the Colorado River trail. Instead of riding the gelding away from the homestead alone – after using the 12-bore Murcott to blast her conniving head off her shoulders.

They rode the wagon, with the black gelding hitched to the tailgate, because neither of the team mares was saddle-broke. And Gold did not relish the prospect of sharing his mount with this girl-woman's nubile body pressed against his.

The only clouds in the sky now were widely scattered: patches of puffy white, flat-bottomed, above the highest ridges in the Mohave Mountains on the Arizona side of the river and the Chemehuevis across in California. The humidity was low now and the heat of the dazzingly bright sun was dry and scorching.

Joanne Engel had foreseen this and when she changed her dress – the fresh one was also gingham-patterned but in green and white – she had donned a plain, wide-brimmed sun hat.

She said it was four miles along the trail to the Gershel place then, for the first quarter of the trip, she was silent: her freckled face as devoid of expression as that of Gold.

Suddenly: 'You dig them all the way up?'

'No.'

'How about cover them up again?'

'No.'

'That's awful . . . leaving them like that.' She sounded genuinely shocked.

'These days I only bury the people I kill, kid.'

'Don't call me kid!' Her anger was venomous.

He said nothing and there was another lengthy silence. During which Barnaby Gold could have reflected upon a different occasion when he drove a wagon similar to this one, with a young girl on the seat beside him. A girl in another kind of trouble. A few years older than Joanne. Her name was Emily Jane and he had married her. She was dead now. Was maybe the reason Barnaby Gold Senior was dead. Certainly her life with the younger Gold and her death away from him was the reason Channon money had been spent to hire the best guns around. Or, rather, his instinctive response to the manner of Emily Jane's death.

He could have been thinking along these lines in the hot silence, but he wasn't. For it was not in his nature to dwell on the past.

'These days?'

'What?'

'You said these days you only – shit, I know! The way you dress and all. You're an undertaker!'

'I used to be.'

'That's creepy.' She shivered, as if for a moment she felt ice cold in the morning heat.

'It's a necessary trade.'

She shook her head. 'I don't mean that. I mean that now – with the guns and all – you kill people and then calmly dig a grave and bury them.'

He could sense her big brown eyes staring at his calm-set profile.

'You do it for money?'

'No.'

Her gaze left his face: to scan their surroundings. The slow flowing river, the dusty trail, the rocky ridges and brush and timber stands. An empty land, suddenly sinister in its desolation. She swallowed hard and all pretence at being an adult was suddenly gone under the pressure of fear.

'Mr Gold, you haven't brought me out here to – '

'Maybe the first man I killed was my father,' he interrupted evenly. 'The second was because – Goddamnit to hell, it's none of your business, kid. Now I only kill people who are aiming to kill me.'

She believed him and her fear was expelled in a long sigh. Which prefixed a silence that remained unbroken until he drove the wagon out of a large stand of mixed timber and another homestead could be seen a half mile along the trail.

'That's the Gershel place.'

Gold had guessed they were getting near their destination when, in the dappled shade of the trees, he sensed a new tension mounting within the girl at his side.

Like the Engel homestead, this one was close to the river bank but the cultivated land was long and narrow rather than square: the four hundred foot wide strip confined by the Colorado on one side and a high, sheer bluff along the other. The crops began almost immediately beyond the timber and the trail made a sharp left turn and then a right one to follow close on the water's edge.

The house and barn, of similar frame construction to those of the Engel place but on a larger scale, were sited back from the river and under the hundred foot high cliff.

A driveway of crushed rock cut away from the trail between symmetrically planted fruit trees and opened out on to the area fronting the house.

A dog began to bark ferociously when the hooves of the team horses and the wheel rims of the wagon sounded on the crushed rock. A man yelled something and the animal became quiet. It was a big black crossbreed, tied with a long rope to the rail of the stoop. Sitting on his haunches and panting from the heat rather than anger, when Gold steered the team into a half-circle to bring the wagon to a halt immediately opposite the front door of the house.

The door was open and a man stood on the threshold.

About fifty, an inch or so over six feet tall and weighing in the region of a beefy two hundred pounds. He was dressed in a heavily soiled bib apron and heavy work boots. No shirt and no hat. What little black hair he had on his head was slicked down over the crown. There was dark stubble on his florid cheeks and pocked jaw. His blue eyes were set in narrow, short sockets that did not match his bulbous nose and fleshy lips.

Dirtied up and unshaven after early hours working his fields, he looked out of place on the swept stoop in the recently white-painted doorframe flanked by shiningly clean windows.

'Mornin' to you, stranger,' he growled, unsmiling. 'Joanne, what you doin' ridin' with a stranger?'

His Tennessee dialect was more pronounced than that of the girl. As he spoke, somebody else moved in the shadowed interior of the house behind him.

'Name's Barnaby Gold, Mr Gershel. Bring you some bad news.'

He hitched the reins around the brake lever and started to swing down from the wagon. Aware of the suspicion in Gershel's hard-set face and of the stone-like posture of Joanne who seemed petrified to the seat. Was still in the process of getting off the wagon when the girl sprang to her feet and shrieked: 'He killed them and raped me!'

Gold had one hand on the seat rail and a boot on the front wheel rim, his back to the man in the doorway. He looked up at the girl as she lunged erect and saw in her face a terror that was only partially spurious: guessed, an instant before she vented the accusation, that she was about to trick him.

He froze, his right hand hanging close to the holstered Peacemaker. Said softly, 'You better tell Mr Gershel you mean Jesse, kid.'

'What?' This from the figure in the shadows behind

Will Gershel. A woman, shock reverberating from the single shrieked word.

Joanne whirled and threw herself off the far side of the wagon, tripped and pitched full-length to the hard packed ground.

'Keep him away from me! Please, don't let him touch me again! He hurt me bad! He killed my mommy and daddy!'

Gold had been within a heartbeat of drawing the big Colt .45. Maybe to blast a bullet into the girl who had reverted to her true age as she vented the indictment. But now, as she scrambled to her feet after moving further away on all fours, he left the gun in the holster: stepped down to the ground and turned to face the Gershels.

He had seen the man was not armed. Now glimpsed Martha behind him and to the side. A well-built woman perhaps ten years the junior of her husband. A good-looking brunette neatly garbed in a black dress and white waist apron. With flour on her hands and a dab of it on her right cheek.

'She's lying, sir . . . lady. Maybe about your boy, Jesse too.'

Martha Gershel's expression was of torment. Will showed high rage. The woman backed into the house, but the man came forward: as Gold crossed to the stoop and stepped up on to it.

'Jesse!'

Joanne's voice did not mask the sound of a footfall and the thumbing back of a gun hammer. Gershel looked to his right and Gold to his left. Saw a young man standing just off the end of the stoop. He wore a similar style apron to his father, with a check shirt beneath it. And a battered Confederate army cap. He held a Purdey bar-in-wood hammer shotgun levelled from the hip. Just one hammer cocked.

'Step aside, Pa! I don't wanna hit you, too!'

He sounded breathless and there was sweat on his thick-featured, acned face. From tension rather than exertion.

'I'll take the chance, boy,' his father said sourly. 'If this here stranger don't unbuckle his gunbelt and hand it to me. If he don't, well you squeeze that trigger, boy. And maybe I won't be around to share in the hell your mother'll let loose for bloodyin' up her clean stoop.'

He did not shift the steady gaze of his small, narrowed eyes away from the expressionless face of Barnaby Gold. And continued to try to outstare the younger man during a long silence broken only by the sobs of Joanne Engel.

'Well, son?'

'He's a killer! He told me! He kills people then buries them!'

'Shut your mouth, Joanne,' Gershel said in the same soured voice. And continued to gaze unblinkingly into Barnaby Gold's face.

'Will I get a fair hearing, sir?'

A slight nod. 'All three of you.'

'Watch him, Mr Gershel! He's got some kind of trick gun on one side! I saw it!'

Gold brought both hands up to his chest and then lowered them slowly to his midriff – half-turning from the waist so that Jesse Gershel could see they came nowhere close to his guns. Then his right hand moved to release the holster ties from around his thigh while the left worked on the buckle.

When the belt was free, he extended it toward Will: all the time poised to lunge into the doorway should the elder Gershel make a sudden move to give his son a clear shot.

Will merely glanced down at the belt as he accepted it. And gave a grunt of approval that perhaps also comprised a sigh of relief. This as he made a move. Not back into the house, though. Instead, he stepped further across the stoop, to put himself completely between Jesse and Gold. Held the gunbelt low down, giving himself no opportunity to draw the holstered Peacemaker or swivel the studded one.

'All right, Jesse,' he said. 'Go put that Purdey back where you found it. And let's us all talk this thing over. Quiet like. With nobody gettin' hot under the collar.'

'Pa, Joanne's folks been shot down by this sonofa-bitch!' Jesse croaked.

'Watch your mouth, boy! With your Ma present!' Then controlled the flare of anger to add evenly: 'She said he killed them. Didn't hear her mention they was shot.'

CHAPTER FOUR

WILL Gershel nodded for Barnaby Gold to enter the house and the black-clad youngster complied with the tacit instruction. Stepped into a square hallway as neat and clean as might be expected from the well-kept exterior of the building.

'Pot of coffee, Martha,' Gershel said as he came in behind. And paused out of habit to wipe his boots on the threshold mat.

The woman, her shock giving way to anxious curiosity, seemed pleased to be offered an escape from the situation. And turned to go through the further of two doors on the right.

'Parlour's first on the left, son. Go on in and sit yourself down.' He raised his voice. 'Girl, come on in the house! Have Mrs Gershel see to where you said you been hurt! Jesse, put the horses in the barn!'

The parlour was perhaps twice as large as that at the Engel homestead. The furniture was of the same plain design and construction, but there was more of it. Rugs on the floor, some pictures on the walls and various ornaments were scattered about. Some good quality china was displayed in a glass-fronted cabinet.

Gold sat down on one of the fan-backed Windsor

chairs at the long central table. Gershel sat at the other end of the table, placed the gunbelt down in front of him.

'Me and Jesse was just in from the fields for coffee, son. So it'll be right up. Don't usually have it in the parlour.'

'Is it all right to smoke, sir?'

'Only allowed in the parlour after supper. Not from these parts, are you?'

'Fairfax, down in the south-east section of the territory for eight years. New York before that.'

'Us Tennessee folks been settled in this neighbourhood for fifteen years. Most of us. Began to move out soon as we knew war was sure to come.'

Two sets of feminine footfalls sounded in the hallway.

'You go into mine and Mr Gershel's bedroom, Joanne. Be with you in a moment.'

'Yes, ma'am.'

The woman entered the parlour carrying a wooden tray on which stood a coffee pot, cream jug, sugar bowl and two cups in saucers. And was embarrassed by a quizzical look from her husband when she set the tray down on the table.

'I just get the best stuff out natural when there's company, Will.'

'Just pour, Martha.'

'As it comes, lady,' Gold said in response to her tacit query.

She filled both cups with black coffee and placed each before a man. Then said, as she went to the door: 'Well, you're talkin' to this young man as if he's an ordinary visitor.'

'Just reckon it'll be better if all the interested parties are present when I hear what happened.'

She paused in the doorway. 'And what about poor Virgil and Mary-Ann?'

'Ain't no doubt but they're dead?' Gershel raised his eyebrows to Gold.

'And half-buried, sir.'

Martha could not quite control a gasp.

'Then there ain't nothin' we can do to help the Engels, Martha.'

She left, her footfalls rapped on the polished floor of the hallway. Then a door closed.

'Somethin' you should know, son.'

'What's that?'

'I don't set no store by what Jesse said about the Engels bein' gunshot to death. I saw it the same way. You carryin' these irons.'

He prodded the gunbelt.

Barnaby Gold clicked his tongue against the roof of his mouth. Then both men sipped their coffee. While a fly buzzed angrily and kept banging against the closed window, seeking escape.

'What you doin' hereabouts?'

'Passing through.'

'We don't usually get your type around here. Up in Bacall sometimes, maybe.'

'My type?'

Another prod at the gunbelt. 'Man who carries this kind of rig, I'd say he knows how to use the irons.'

'I'm learning, sir.'

Jesse Gershel had made a lot of noise in taking the wagon and horses around to the rear of the house. Now he clumped in loudly through the rear door. His footfalls sounded sullen, which was how his acned face looked when he entered the parlour.

'You want coffee, you'll have to bring a cup, boy.'

'I don't want coffee, Pa! I want to know what he done to Joanne Engel!'

He glared his hostility at Gold, then dropped into a

padded rocker to one side of the fireplace. And clasped the arms so tightly his knuckles showed white.

The bedroom door across the hall opened and Will Gershel started. 'Reckon we're goin' to find that out . . . '

'You animal!' Martha snarled as she appeared on the threshold of the parlour, her cheeks pale and her lips quivering. 'What kind of man are you to do that to a mere child?'

She was holding something in both hands. A piece of fabric, pink and white in colour. Barnaby Gold shifted his gaze away from Jesse, who looked as anguished as his mother, and recognised what it was Martha was holding. Before she displayed it by extending it forward and allowing it to unfurl. The tattered remains of the gingham dress that Joanne had donned after changing from her nightgown. But instead of just the one tear, it now had many. From neckline to waist at the front, from hem to waist at the side, some lesser damage at the back and one sleeve almost ripped off.

'It had to be while I was washing up in her parents' bedroom,' Gold said.

'I'll tell you when it's time to have your say,' Will Gershel growled, and punctuated the words with the click of the hammer being thumbed back on the wood-butted Peacemaker.

Gold merely glanced at the man holding one of his own guns on him. Then returned his attention to the doorway, where Joanne had moved up, head bowed and hands clasped in front of her, beside Martha.

'The poor child had the presence of mind to put this back on under a fresh dress, Will.'

'She hurt like she said?'

His wife tossed the ruined dress on to a small table just inside the doorway and nodded. Was embarrassed again as she looked between Will and Jesse.

'We ain't drinkin' in no bar, woman! Ain't none of us goin' to get no evil pleasure from what you say.'

Martha stared at the fly that was still attempting vainly to penetrate the window. 'Bruises here and here. And here. Scratches here and here. Some blood down here that isn't from any cut. Even teeth marks here.'

She used just one hand to indicate on her own fine body where the marks showed on the adolescent flesh of Joanne Engel. First both shoulders and buttocks. Then the breasts. Next the thighs. Finally low down on the belly, from one hip to the other.

'Kill him, Pa, kill him!' Jesse groaned tearfully.

'He hurt me real bad, Mr Gershel,' the girl added, head still bowed. 'But not for that. He has to pay for what he done to my mommy and daddy. He shot them down in cold blood. Then he done these things to me while they was dead in the next room.'

Barnaby Gold ignored Jesse and Joanne. To hold Will Gershel's steady gaze. His hands lay on the tabletop, thumbs hooked beneath it. Ready to hurl it upwards at the merest hint that the man holding the gun was about to squeeze the trigger.

'Ain't no sense in my Martha makin' all that up, son.'

'No point in me bringing the girl here if I'd – '

'Why you done that is why I didn't allow Jesse to blast you full of shot.'

Gershel nodded twice as he said this, then looked across at his son. Barnaby Gold loosened his grip on the edge of the table but left his hands there. Also looked toward Jesse and could still not be totally certain he was the young man who rode away from the Engel homestead in such a hurry. The rider had not been wearing a bib apron and a CSA forage cap.

'It was the first time you ever stayed away from home all night, boy.'

'Will!' Martha snapped, angry and anxious.

Jesse swallowed hard. 'Like I already told you, Pa! I was drinking in the Riverside Hotel! The people there will tell you I was! I had one or two more than I should've. Ridin' home, I felt sick to my stomach. Stopped to rest and just fell asleep.'

Gershel was looking back at Gold again and now he nodded. 'You told me, boy. And now the stranger here has heard you. Knows you claim there are folks in town can back up that you was drinkin' in the hotel till late. You wanna tell your version now, son?'

Gold did so and Gershel looked away from him only once – to glance at his wife when the young man at the other end of the table took out a cheroot and lit it. But the houseproud Martha did not break her concentration on what was being said. Gold left the cheroot tin open on the table and dropped the dead match and then ash into its lid.

'I didn't!' Joanne cried from the doorway beside Martha Gershel as soon as Gold was finished. 'I didn't say that about Jesse! When he'd hurt me that way he started to ask me things! About if I had a boy and all! I told him me and Jesse was kinda walking out! He asked me where Jesse lived and I told him! He said he didn't want to leave me home with my dead folks! He said he'd bring me here! But that I wasn't to say what happened! To say that mommy and daddy hadn't come home! Only after he'd gone was I to tell you what really happened, Mr Gershel! If I said anything while he was still here, he'd kill me! And you and Mrs Gershel and Jesse, too!'

She blurted out the denials so fast that many of the words ran together. And she was breathless at the end of it. Sagged against Martha, who encircled her shoulders with a supporting and comforting arm.

Will Gershel listened to her stoically without looking

at her, his eyes and the gun still concentrating on Barnaby Gold – who revealed no facial response to what the girl was saying.

'Like you to stub out that cheroot, son. And put your arms down at your sides. Jesse, you go out to the barn and bring enough rope to tie the stranger to his chair.'

'What you goin' to do, Will?' Martha asked fearfully.

'Get some help, woman. The killin' of Virgil and Mary-Ann and what's been done to the girl . . . it's too big for us to handle alone.'

Jesse was already on his way to do his father's bidding. Joanne tried to meet his eyes as he went past her, but he pointedly avoided this. Gold continued to smoke.

'You goin' to take him to Sheriff Polk?'

Gershel grunted and scowled. 'You know that ain't our way, woman! This is country trouble. No business of Floyd Polk.'

Once out of the house, Jesse must have run to the barn and back again. There was a triumphant smile on his face until he came by his mother and Joanne to re-enter the parlour.

'You want to take a leak or anythin'?' Gershel asked.

'No.'

'All right. Now you best do what I told you.' He got up from his chair and moved along the side of the table. 'Or I'll put a bullet in a kneecap. Hear tell that's real painful.'

Martha gasped.

Barnaby Gold crushed out the cheroot and dropped his arms to his sides. 'Okay. Just wish you believed me as much as I believe you.'

CHAPTER FIVE

THE rope was coiled four times around his chest and arms to hold him to the back of the chair and three times around his thighs and the seat.

Jesse did this, breathing hard as if it required a great deal of effort, while Martha took Joanne back to the bedroom, insisting she should rest.

Will watched in silence and, after Gold was secured in the chair, slotted the Peacemaker back in the holster and took the gunbelt off the table.

Then: 'Be back in three or maybe four hours at the most, stranger. Reckon you're goin' to get mighty uncomfortable, but we don't have anywhere on the place to just lock you in. Where you couldn't get out of. Ain't no use tellin' you not to worry. Can just say other folks will give you as fair a hearin' as I have.'

Barnaby Gold clicked his tongue.

Gershel shook his head, puzzled. 'You're a strange one and no mistake, son.'

'It's been said before.'

'Let's go, Pa.'

'One thing, Mr Gershel.'

'Yeah?'

'Appreciate it if you'd see he took proper care of my horse.'

Gershel nodded and started for the door, carrying the gunbelt.

'It ain't your horse I got anythin' against!' Jesse snarled.

'Don't kick a man when he's down, boy!' his father said with equal anger.

'That's when it's easiest to do,' Gold murmured as the man and boy went into the hallway, out of earshot.

The term 'strange one' and many similar expressions had been used about Barnaby Gold ever since childhood. At free school in New York City. During the six years he worked with his father in the funeral parlour there, and then in the small town of Fairfax and the neighbouring larger community of Standing.

Strange because he was like no other child or young man of his age that those he came into contact with had ever met. An outsider who appeared to enjoy only his own company: always seemed to be detached from his surroundings, even in a crowd. A personality so solitary that he gave the impression of being aloof. Which acted to irritate certain people who were not prepared to accept such a misfit in their society.

At school there had been fights. Totally one-sided for a long time, while Barnaby Gold took his unwarranted punishment – convinced he was not good at juvenile brawling. Until one winter's night with his mother recently dead and his father drunk, he responded to an impulse to retaliate. Lashed out at those parts of his opponent's body where he could remember being hurt the most.

Soon there was to be another confrontation. This time in cold blood, to test that his first victory had not been a matter of luck. It had not, and Barnaby Gold won the right to be left alone by his contemporaries. To read a great deal, to stand on the waterfront and gaze out across the ocean beyond which lay Europe and to develop a natural ability for working with timber.

He was aware of the puzzled comments passed by adults about him – some of them addressed to his father – but he paid no heed to them. Either back in New York City or in the more confined society of the small towns of Arizona. Where he discovered he enjoyed horse riding, so became good at it. And game shooting with the Murcott. Whoring with the Mexican girls in the cantina at Standing.

He had a great deal of luck when he first had to use a revolver to kill a man. But since then he had indulged in many practice sessions as he crossed the deserts and mountains, leaving a clear trail for the hired gunslingers to follow. And had long since recovered from the surprise of finding out that he took to handguns as instinctively as, years before, he had discovered his talent for wood working.

And that, after the first time, to kill people bothered him not at all.

But here in the comfortably furnished parlour of the Gershel house, none of his practical skills were of any use to him as he sat trapped to the chair: hearing the fly as it sought escape from the room and the small sounds made by Martha doing chores in the kitchen.

What he was able to do was twist his right wrist and wriggle his hands into the side pocket of his pants. Ease open the box of matches in there and take them out one at a time. Strike each one on the edge of the chair seat and hold it so that the flame could eat into the rope at the top of his thigh. Aware of the danger that the rope could flare and catch his clothing alight.

The rope was a quarter-way burnt through and there were six dead, charred matchsticks on the floor beside the chair when Martha Gershel's footfalls rapped in the hallway. She pointedly avoided looking in through the open door of the parlour before she went off to the bedroom.

'Not asleep yet, my dear?'

'It's hard, Mrs Gershel.' There was pain and misery in the girl's tone. 'Knowing that awful man is in the house.'

'He can't harm you, Joanne. Not any more. You try to sleep now. You'll feel much better when you wake up.'

'Yes, ma'am.'

The door closed and this time the woman did pause to glance in at Barnaby Gold, her good-looking face wearing a scowl of revulsion. But her sniff was not of the disdainful kind and Gold knew she had caught the acrid taint of burnt rope. Using the cover of the tabletop, he tried to part his legs, but too many fibres of the rope were still intact.

Martha Gershel came into the parlour. Determined, then anxious as she neared the table. Her hands were clean of the flour now, but the grains were still daubed on her cheek. Her face was sheened with sweat.

'I only allow Will to smoke his pipe in here after supper,' she said quickly. And just as quickly moved up to the table, leaned across with both hands and dragged the cup and saucer and the opened cheroot tin from in front of Gold. Then her attitude was of relief when she had placed them on the tray with the cup and saucer her husband had used at the far end of the table. Her eyes poured scorn and hatred on him as she said, 'They'll maybe allow you one more smoke before they hang you. So I'll keep these things safe.'

'Appreciate it.'

Some of the high emotion drained out of her. 'They will hang you, you know. You bein' what you are. And Jesse and Joanne and her folks bein' like us. Ordinary, decent folks. I won't agree with it. Not that you shouldn't hang for what you done. But the law should do it. Proper, with whatever kind of dignity there can be in such a thing.'

'Appreciate what you say, lady.'

'Well, you're some mother's son.'

'Like Jesse.'

She stiffened. 'Our kind ain't killers and . . . and rapists! Why, Jesse got treated like a son by Mary-Ann and Virgil any time he went over to their place. Same way we treat Joanne. And them two children, they're promised to each other. Just as soon as the girl's of age to marry. That's one mountain custom we didn't bring out West. Girl gotta be sixteen or more before she's allowed to marry and . . . and be taken by a man.'

Gold had the impression that, when Martha Gershel spoke of rape and a woman being taken by a man, she experienced a surge of excitement. He judged this from the way her eyes brightened and her grip tightened on the tray.

'So the fair hearing talk was crap, lady?'

She flinched when he used the mild expletive. 'Around here we do things right, stranger! And it ain't right to use foul language in the hearin' of a female!'

'My apologies, lady. Wrong of me to assume that just because the Engel girl has a bad mouth that every . . .'

'I've never even heard that sweet girl take the Lord's name in vain!' she countered, then whirled and strode from the room, the china on the tray rattling.

Gold waited until he could hear her washing the dirty crockery before he struck another match. Then another and another.

Martha Gershel had completed her dish washing chore and had left the house by the rear door before he saw the rope was burned through sufficiently to snap with a hard tug. And he was about to give this a try when he heard a small sound and wrenched up his head to look toward the doorway. Where Joanne Engel stood, her shoes off so that he had not heard her tread across the hall.

'Martha's out to the barn doing something, Barnaby,' the girl said, displaying her slightly buck teeth in a gentle smile. Once more acting the part of a full grown woman, in her juvenile attire of gingham dress and white socks with her hair in pigtails.

She turned sideways on to him, back to the doorframe and one leg raised and bent with the sole of the foot pressed to the woodwork. And she was arched forward a little, to thrust out her underdeveloped breasts.

Gold clicked his tongue.

'I don't know what, but it could be she's doing something to herself. I heard her talking to you awhile back. I reckon she hates you as much as you hate me, Barnaby. But it sounded like she lusts after you, too. When she was talking about – '

'Beat it, kid.'

Anger coloured her freckled cheeks and injected rigidity into her alluring stance. 'I told you before, don't call me that!'

'What other kind of shit can you stir for me, kid?'

She dropped the folded-up foot to the floor and swung away from the doorframe to face him full on.

'I was maybe willing to help you, you sonofabitch! Cut you loose so you maybe had a chance of getting away from these rubes around here!'

She came into the room, her rage not so all-consuming that she failed to remember Martha Gershel was close by. So she kept her voice to a venomous, rasping whisper.

'But now I'm going to watch you swing from a tree branch. And I'm going to get a real thrill out of doing that. Especially since I'll know you're dancing on that rope for something you didn't do. That'll make it even better, you high nosed bastard. And you'll know that if you hadn't treated me like I was just out of diapers, you maybe would've missed being lynched.'

She was at the side of the table, her hands splayed on its top, half-leaning across it to bring her flushed face within a foot of Gold's. He could feel the hot breath of her anger on his skin.

Just one length of rope had been used to secure the prisoner. An end was tied to a leg of the chair and it was simply wound around his thighs then his torso and arms and fastened with a running knot close to the top of the chair back. So that it only had to be parted anywhere along its length and he was free.

'Emily Jane and Maria were women.'

'What?'

'Married one and the other was a whore. Both of them screwed me up real bad. You're just a kid, but in that department you leave them way behind.'

'I told you, don't call me – '

She snatched up one of her hands and made to lash it at his face.

He jerked his thighs apart and the section of charred rope snapped. He powered upright and the coils of the rope fell away. Except where it encircled his chest. Then the act of shooting forward an arm to grasp her wrist caused the knot to run.

The chair fell to the floor.

Joanne Engel screamed her terror.

He used his free hand to raise the rope noose up over his shoulders and head. His hat fell off.

Her scream continued.

He dropped the noose over her head, released his hold on her wrist and jerked the knot tight to the nape of her neck. The sound she was making was choked to a premature end.

'Be a pleasure to kill you, kid,' he whispered, close to her ear. 'But I don't get my thrills like that.'

The rear door of the house banged open and running footfalls came from the kitchen.

'Joanne!'

Martha Gershel sounded anxious, but not overly concerned.

Barnaby Gold kept the noose tight enough around the girl's neck to keep her silent, but not to choke her: as he gathered her up with an arm around her waist and carried her struggling form to the parlour doorway.

The woman emerged from the kitchen and stopped short, suddenly brought to the edge of hysteria. She was carrying the gunbelt.

Joanne Engel saw her and was still. And for a heartbeat, so was the woman. But then she moved her hand toward the studded Peacemaker – had her thumb on the hammer and was about to swivel the muzzle toward Gold when his voice caused her to freeze.

'Try it and I'll throw this lying little bitch at you, lady! And keep hold of my end of the rope!'

Martha Gershel's fine breasts heaved with tension. Her eyes looked ready to pop out of their sockets.

'What's happened?' she gasped.

'Let go of the gun and toss the belt over here, lady.'

'I can't.'

Joanne was trying to say something and he allowed a little slack in the rope.

'I don't want to die, ma'am!' she blurted huskily. 'Please do like he – '

'I can't trust you not to – '

Barnaby Gold looked calmly into the mask of horror that was her face. Said: 'Way you want it, lady.'

'No!' She shrieked the single syllable and hurled the gunbelt across the hallway. Hard enough so that he felt a sharp pain when the butt of one of the guns hit his knee.

Then he simply let go of the rope and uncurled his arm

from around the girl's waist. It was not a long fall, but she did not expect it. And there was no time to prepare for the impact. She screamed as her hip, elbow, shoulder and the side of her head cracked against the floor.

Gold went down on to his haunches, took hold of the gunbelt and stood up.

'You stinking, rotten – '

'Watch your mouth, kid,' Gold cut in on her evenly, as he began to buckle the belt. 'There is a lady present.'

Martha sagged against the kitchen doorframe. 'Dear God,' she whispered, a hand at her throat. 'I just thought the girl was havin' a nightmare.'

Gold finished tying the knot to hold the toe of the holster to his thigh. Asked: 'Were you going to blast her demons away with these .45s, lady?'

'No, I . . . '

He retreated into the parlour, to pick up his hat from the floor. Then took the time to go to the window, open it and let out the fly. The dog, which was lying flat out in the shade, growled at the sight of him.

Out in the hallway, the girl had crawled toward the woman, who was still as Gold had left her, sagged against the kitchen doorframe.

'I think you went to get these guns to kill me, Mrs Gershel.'

She swallowed hard. Then used a great deal of effort to pull herself erect. 'That's exactly right, stranger! To get it over and done with. Make it quick for you. And so the decent, hard-working men around this neighbourhood wouldn't have to carry the guilt of a lynchin' around with them for the rest of their lives.'

There was pride and defiance in her certainty that what she had planned was the right thing to do. And then she placed a protective arm around the shoulders of Joanne again after the girl had risen painfully to her feet.

Both of them backed fearfully into the kitchen when Gold started toward them.

'You took my cheroots, lady.'

She nodded toward a small pine, scrubbed-top table against a wall of the kitchen which was as neat and clean as the other parts of the house Gold had seen. His tin of cheroots, still open with the match, ash and remains of a smoke in the lid, was on the tray on the table. He emptied this mess on to the floor and took out a cheroot before placing the tin in an inside pocket of the frock coat. Then crossed to the range and used a match from a box on a shelf above to light the tobacco. He also pocketed the box.

Went toward the open rear door of the house.

'I'm grateful, stranger,' Martha Gershel said.

'Why you thanking him, ma'am?' Joanne asked, her voice shrill and on the brink of anger.

'He could have spilled worse than that, child. And taken more than a handful of matches from us.'

Barnaby Gold ignored the girl to direct a lingering look at the woman. The kind of look – arrogantly appraising – which a young man in his mid-twenties did not normally offer to a woman of more than forty.

The old-for-her-age Joanne Engel recognised what was implied by this open gaze from the cool green eyes of the black-clad man. And scowled her resentment.

While Martha's cheeks became flushed in a manner that would have better suited the girl.

'Under different circumstances, lady, there's something here I'm sure I would have enjoyed having.' He nodded, then added: 'Bye-bye.'

CHAPTER SIX

THE big black dog barked at him as he rode the gelding around the side of the house and across the yard to the strip of crushed rock through the trees. Barked and lunged at him, then snarled through bared teeth each time the rope snapped taut and jerked him to a halt. He could hear the animal for several minutes after he had ridden out of sight of the two pairs of eyes which had gazed fixedly at him from the stoop-shaded threshold of the house. One pair hating him, the other filled with a strange mixture of doubt, regret and subdued excitement.

Although he did not know of these expressions: was merely conscious of being watched from behind. Until he was on the trail beside the river, heading north and the fruit tree orchard hid him from the house.

He felt no hatred toward Joanne Engel or regret at having allowed himself to be led so willingly into the trap that the Gershels had closed around him. What was done was done – he was as green as spring grass in a damp climate. But he learned from each new experience in the so far harsh world outside the confines of Fairfax and Standing. Maybe the hard way, but that was probably the best way.

He smoked the cheroot down to a stub and tossed this

into the Colorado River. By which time he was a mile beyond the Gershel property and riding through a stand of pinyon, juniper and oaks much more extensive than that to the south: filling a broad valley that had opened out from the end of the riverside bluff that crowded the homestead back down the trail.

Deep in the timber, the foliage of which offered pleasant shade from the blazing sun that was nearing its midday peak, he reached a clearing and reined in the gelding. The cleared area, some two acres, was man-made by the felling of trees over a number of years. The oldest stumps, many of them rotted, were closest to the river bank. And some of these first-to-be-felled trees had been used to construct a northern-style log cabin far enough back from the water's edge to escape flooding when the river was swollen by rain.

Two shade oaks had been left growing at the front corners of the cabin. Out back of it there was a high pile of cordwood cut to even lengths and parked beside this a two-wheeled pushcart. On the eastern side of the clearing a half dozen recently-felled trees lay sprawled out from their yellow-topped stumps. Two had already been cleaned of branches, which were smouldering with a great deal of smoke on a tidily-built bonfire. While a man was working with a bucking saw and a small broad axe to strip another, tossing the severed trimmings on to the fire.

A tall, broadly-built, muscular man wearing only a pair of denim pants and calked boots: was hatless despite the strong sunlight that poured down, unobstructed, into the clearing.

The logger had his back to Barnaby Gold and was a rather indistinct form through the lazily drifting smoke of the fire. The thud of the axe, the rasp of the saw and the crackling of the sap-moist timber on the fire acted to mask the thud of hooves on the sun-browned grass of the clearing until the mounted man had ridden through the smoke and was within twenty feet of the naked-to-the-waist man. Who whistled tunelessly while he worked.

'Good morning to you, sir.'

Gold spoke as he reined in the gelding during a pause when the logger dropped the saw to pick up the axe.

The whistling was abruptly curtailed and for a full second the man remained in a frozen stoop. Gold delved a hand into the holed pocket on the left side of his coat and gripped the mother-of-pearl butt of the studded .45. But his green eyes were lit with a personable smile when the man whirled toward him, axe held in an aggressive, cross-body position.

'Shit, kid, what's the big idea?'

He was in his fifties – maybe even early sixties. He had long, greasy black hair like an Indian, framing a face stained to a darker shade of brown than his heavily haired torso: the flesh inscribed with countless deep lines where it was exposed above his thickly growing grey and black beard. There was resentful anger in his light blue eyes and the way his discoloured teeth showed between lips all but concealed by the beard and its accompanying moustache.

'Uh?'

The logger lowered the axe and half-sat on the tree he was trimming: ran a hirsute forearm over his face to clean off most of the sweat beads hanging in the cracks of his skin.

'One thing I can't abide is bein' crept up on.'

Gold maintained his grip on the gun but did not thumb back the hammer. With a jerk of his right thumb over his shoulder he indicated the half-width of the clearing behind him.

'Rode my horse from there to here, sir. Can't see that as creeping.'

'And I've spent best part of sixty-one years listenin' to bigger brutes than these saplings crashin' down, kid. Which ain't done my hearin' any good at all.'

'I beg your pardon, sir.'

'And don't call me, sir. I ain't been bull of the woods for a long time. Name's John Lloyd Larkin. The hill-billies around here call me just JL. What can I do for you, kid?'

The alarm at being startled had gone and now he was peering with curiosity at his visitor: and it was obvious that his sight as well as his hearing was impaired.

'Not a thing. I'm just passing through. Needed to be sure you wouldn't try to stop me.'

Larkin had examined him from head to toe, then started to check on his horse and gear. 'You're the guy Will Gershel says might have killed the Engels and screwed that snot-nose kid of theirs?'

'You going to try to stop me, Mr Larkin?'

The logger spat and some of the saliva did not clear his beard. 'Shit, kid, how would I do that? You with them two pistols and that sawn-down shotgun dangling from the saddle?'

Gold nodded. 'Okay.'

He took his hand from the coat pocket and took up the reins.

'You have to do anythin' to that girl and Mrs Gershel to get free?'

'The girl may have a rope burn around her neck.'

'If I'm gonna believe that, I have to figure you didn't do what the girl said you did.'

'You're a believer in truth, Mr Larkin.'

'Then ride away from here in any direction but north, kid. Will Gershel's a good and honest man. If he wasn't, he'd have took care of you himself. Seein' as how you claim Jesse, his own son, did the killin's. But with the crowd of other hillbillies he's roundin' up, he'll take a back seat. Good and honest men, nearly all of them. But in a crowd, they'll stick together to protect their own. Wrongs and rights of it won't make much odds. You ride on the north trail and you'll head slap bang into them.'

'They told you a lot, Mr Larkin,' Gold lit another cheroot, 'considering you're not one of them.'

'No, kid, I ain't one of them. I'm from Illinois and spent most of my workin' life up in Montana and Oregon until I got too old to keep pace with the youngsters. And my blood got too thin to take them northern winters. But Will and me, we get on fine, us bein' such close neighbours. And he asked me a favour. To go down the trail to his place and stand guard over you. Didn't like the idea of leavin' Martha to do it. But with so many men to get together over a big piece of country, it needed him and Jesse both to round them up.'

'Why didn't you do him the favour, Mr Larkin?'

'Said I'd think about it, kid. Kept thinkin' instead of how I saw Jesse last night. Ridin' south real fast. How he didn't look sick from liquor to me. And how, if he got sick of a sudden, he was close enough to home to make it. Instead of beddin' down in the timber.'

'But you didn't say anything, right?'

A shake of the head. 'No, kid. On account of I'm an old man who likes to eat regular. And likes workin' in the timber to earn my bread. But if the people hereabouts started to cut their own stove wood . . . well . . . ?'

'Sure, Mr Larkin.'

'Course, kid, if I was asked right out, I wouldn't lie about what I seen.'

'Bye-bye, Mr Larkin.'

He clucked to the horse and tugged gently on the reins to head him across the clearing toward the point where the north trail led into the timber.

'I advised you against goin' that way, kid!' the logger called after him.

'Appreciate it,' Gold acknowledged, and leaned to the side, to flick the partially-smoked cheroot into the fire: a scowl on his face as if the tobacco had suddenly started to taste bad.

And felt the tug of a bullet snag at his coat sleeve. At the same instant as he heard the crack of a rifle. An instant before John Lloyd Larkin grunted and rasped: 'Shit, some bastard shot me.'

CHAPTER SEVEN

BARNABY Gold kicked free of the left stirrup and straightened his right leg, using the leverage of his right foot in the stirrup to power a headlong leap from the saddle. The gelding, calm in the wake of the sudden gunshot, was alarmed by the abrupt actions of his rider. Reared and bolted.

Gold slammed hard to the ground and grunted with the pain of the impact.

'Hillbilly sonsofbitches!' Larkin shrieked.

And as Gold forced himself into a fast roll through the drifting smoke of the fire he caught a glimpse of the logger. Who had stood up and picked up his axe to carry on working as the younger man made to leave. And by so doing had placed his naked torso in the line of fire of the rifle. So that when Gold unwittingly ducked to throw away his cheroot at the moment the sniper squeezed his trigger, the bullet zeroed in on a fresh target – the centre of the hirsute chest of Larkin. Who, as Gold rolled over and over through the smoke, dropped his axe, clutched both big hands to the bloodied area beneath his beard, and twisted to the ground.

'Gold, you lousy shithead!' the sniper shrieked, his dismayed tone at the misplaced shot almost a perfect match for that which sounded in the dying curse of Larkin.

Another shot cracked out and the gelding skidded to a halt on the bank of the river. It was a wild one, fired in anger, that exploded chips of bark from the side of a stump. Several yards wide of where Gold traded the insubstantial cover of the smoke for the solidness of the felled tree upon which Larkin had been working.

His leap over the tree and into its cover was seen by the sniper: invited a third shot that came much closer to the intended target.

'You ain't gonna get away this time, Gold! Your luck's almost run out! You wanna start countin' your last breaths?'

The black-clad young man heard the lever action of the repeater pumped while the sniper was issuing his threat. And had bellied several feet along the trunk before the fourth shot sounded. Exploding a bullet into the trunk at the point where he had first dived into cover.

He was amongst the untrimmed foliage by then, and made a turn to edge away from it: aware that his movements might cause the lighter branches to tremble and reveal his position.

He knew exactly where the sniper was positioned – in a tree, perhaps fifteen feet above the ground to the right of where the north trail ran into the timber. Thought it likely that the man's elevated vantage point had only a narrow angle view of the clearing, confined by the foliage which served to hide him.

'You were crazy to think you could ever get away with what you done, Gold! You never had a snowball's chance in Hades, shithead! And I'll see to it you get yours, kid! And if you run, boy, it won't bother me none havin' to blast a hole in your back!'

Barnaby Gold listened impassively to the string of

taunts and threats. Aware that the man was not yelling to hear himself: for although his voice acted to cover the sounds of creaking branches, it also served to tell Gold that the sniper was climbing down from the tree. Each phrase vented from a position closer to the ground.

The yelling continued and Barnaby Gold took the chance that the sniper was paying more attention to keeping his footing than to whatever area of the clearing he could see. And he raised up on to all fours and went over three more felled trees. Then plunged into the prickly brush of the surrounding timber that Larkin would never get to cut down.

Thorns snagged at his clothes and tore the flesh on the back of his right hand. He protected his face with a forearm, but felt the warmth of blood on his legs as they were barbed through his pants in several places: this as he pushed deeper into the timber. Far enough to be concealed by the vicious brush: but still within earshot of the smallest sounds out on the sunlit area.

The trickling of the river, the crackling of the fire and the sounds of his gelding at the water's edge, drinking. The sounds of his own breathing and even his heartbeats had greater volume in his ears. After the man intent upon killing him had ceased to shout.

He was standing erect now, facing the clearing that was hidden to his expressionless green eyes. Right hand raised to his mouth, gently sucking at the blood oozing from the torn skin on its back. Left fisted around the eagle-butted Peacemaker, forefinger to the unguarded trigger and thumb on the hammer. Barrel still pointed to the ground.

More than a full minute ticked into history during which the sniper made no sound – intentional or otherwise – to betray his continued presence.

There was not, in Barnaby Gold's attitude or expression, the least sign that he did not possess the brand of patience that would enable him to stand there in unmoving silence for an infinite number of minutes.

'Gold?'

Some insects which had started to buzz were silenced by the shout.

'Gold, you sonofabitch! They say you reckon yourself a real hotshot with them two guns of yours! Are you that, boy?'

He sounded like he was from one of the Southern states, but his accent was not so downhome Tennessee as that of the Gershels, or even Joanne Engel.

'So why don't you face up to it like a man? Face to face? What do you say, boy?'

The insects were buzzing again, no longer concerned by the shouting voice.

'Maybe you're as good as they say! So you get a chance! I'll toss away this here rifle! Count on three and I'll step out into the open! Colt in the holster! Pace it out until one of us thinks he can drop the other! What do you say, boy?'

Gold looked at the back of his hand. The wound had stopped seeping blood and the lips were clean.

Something thudded heavily to the ground close to where the sniper was standing.

'There goes the rifle, boy! You ready? One . . . two . . . three!'

Gold blew out of the side of his mouth to shift a fly off his cheek.

'Frig you, Gold!' For the first time, there was a note of fear in the man's voice. Which he recognised himself. And tried to negate with a harsh laugh. 'So you don't want to play it my way! Well, if you can see me, you can see I ain't dumb! It was just a piece of tree branch I tossed away!'

Gold clicked his tongue against the roof of his mouth.

'And I'm comin' to get you! Because I know you can't be too far away from where I last saw you. And I figure I'll spot you and you'll have an extra hole in your body long before I'm close enough for any hand-gunslinger!'

Gold jutted out his lower lip and blew a draught of cool air over his sweat-sheened face. More than half a minute had gone before he first heard the setting down of a booted foot in the clearing. Then another and another. Slow and measured. The strides long. Advancing to within perhaps forty feet of where Larkin was sprawled at the side of the felled trees and the fire. Then crabwise to keep outside of effective revolver range.

Then the man cracked: 'All right, you shithead!' He fired a shot. 'If you ain't dead already . . . ' Another shot. ' . . . then your time's up now!'

He lunged into a run as he shrieked the words and exploded shot after shot. Coming fast through the drifting smoke toward the felled trees against which his bullets were impacting.

Gold clicked his tongue to mark off each shot as it was jacked from the magazine of the rifle and blasted from the muzzle. And he began his move as the last but one shell was levered into the breech, the stirring of the brush covered by running footfalls, shrieked obscenities and the sounds of the gun being prepared to fire, then fired.

The eagle-butted Peacemaker was swivelled on its stud to be levelled from the hip and he protected his face with his right forearm. The sting of the older wounds in his legs was negated by the sharper pains of new tears in the skin. The heel of his right hand was scratched from the base of the finger to the wrist.

' . . . friggin' shithead bastard sonofabitchin' . . . '

The final bullet exploded from the rifle and sprayed splinters of bark over the unfeeling face of John Lloyd Larkin.

Gold had simply taken a chance, after seven shells were exploded, that the sniper's repeater was a Winchester. Sheriff Walt Glazer of Standing, with whom he had hunted in the past, owned a Winchester. Most men's repeaters were Winchesters. With a magazine capacity of twelve shells. Now, as Barnaby Gold lunged out of the brush and came to a halt, the sniper whirled into a half-turn, pumped the lever action to send a spent shellcase spinning through the air, and squeezed the trigger.

'You're fresh out, mister.'

The range was ten feet, the man clear of the smoke from the fire but standing in a pall of acrid-smelling vapour from exploded black powder. A man who matched Gold's six feet and was just a little fleshier. Five or six years older, though. With prematurely whitened hair. Narrow-eyed with finely chiseled features. Dressed all in dark blue – Stetson, kerchief, shirt and pants. With just the one revolver, in a holster tied down to his left thigh.

Younger, and not so heavily built as Gold had visualised from listening to him.

The moment Gold emerged from the brush, he dropped his bloodied right hand to expose his left and the swivelled gun it was fisted around. He kept his right hand there, holding back the side of the coat.

'I'll kill you or you can carry a message, mister.'

His words were softer and more measured than when he first spoke to the man. Now that the Winchester had clicked empty and the man who held it was contemplating his chances of hurling it toward Gold and going for the holstered Army Colt.

'What?' He continued to hold the rifle aimed at Gold. The deep fear in his eyes easing a little as their gaze flicked from the youthful face to the levelled Peacemaker and back again.

'Where's your horse?'

He half-turned his head to indicate the direction from which he had come. 'Up the trail a ways.'

'Throw the rifle on the fire. Then take the revolver from the holster and toss it into the timber.'

'You ain't gonna shoot me down like you did . . . ?'

'Appreciate it if you'd do as you're told without asking questions, mister.'

'Why should I trust you?' He swallowed hard.

Barnaby Gold clicked his tongue. 'Your rifle is all shot out. Your revolver is still in the holster. Why shouldn't I shoot you now?'

'Shit, that's right.' He allowed a small smile of relief to cross his features. But seemed to consider this a sign of weakness. And his expression became hard-set as he did what he was told with the Winchester. Then he eased the Colt from his holster by holding the butt between the thumb and forefinger of his left hand. He let it dangle at his side. 'Them fancy quick shootin' swivel guns can spin a man around, you know that?'

'Did me, the first time I used it. I've got the hang of it now. The message isn't all that important, mister.'

'Hey, wait!' Gold's icy implacability aroused fresh fear in the man: who slowly drew back his left arm, then swung it forward. To arc the revolver into the brush behind Gold.

'Okay. Now you go to your horse and you ride back up the trail. And tell your buddies I'm out of the Gershel house. But the woman and girl are fine. You tell them what happened here. About how you killed Larkin by accident. Which is a damn shame for me. Because he saw Jesse Gershel ride by this place last night looking not at all sick.'

The man listened hard, his head cocked to one side in an attitude of puzzlement.

'Can you remember all that, mister?'

A vigorous nod. 'Sure. Sure, Gold.'

The younger man's nod was less frantic. And he clicked his tongue. 'Recently I've taken up killing any man who tries to kill me, mister. Turning you loose, because maybe it might help to convince the people around here I didn't do what I'm accused of at the Engel house.'

'Sure, sure, I get it.' He did not look like he understood what was being said to him. Was just anxious to get out of the clearing and away from the levelled Peacemaker. 'I'll leave now, all right?'

'Keep one thing in mind.'

'What?'

'If I get to hear you turned this thing around.' He made a sideways gesture with his head to indicate the slumped body of Larkin. 'Tell your buddies it was me instead of you who killed him – I'll bury you. And to hell with the consequences. Bye-bye.'

The man blinked. 'What?'

'I said bye-bye.'

'Sure, sure!'

He whirled and began to walk quickly across the clearing. Then broke into a run.

Barnaby Gold did not watch him. He let go of his coat and the gun and moved to where his hat lay on the ground, displaced from his head when he plunged off the gelding. Then he walked slowly toward where his horse was cropping at grass on the bank of the river. He sucked at the new wound on his right hand.

While he was mounting, he heard the man curse a horse into movement: then the thud of galloping hooves, the sound diminishing through the timber. He lit a cheroot and started in the same direction. Not sparing a glance for the remains of the unfortunate John Lloyd Larkin who had died so tragically and uselessly. For, as an undertaker, Gold had needed to become hardened to the fact of death. Which was inevitably tragic and futile unless the deceased and the bereaved had the strength of religious belief to give it reason.

And neither, as he rode into the pleasant shade of the timber, did he reflect upon what the man ahead of him was likely to do. Deliver the message as given and be grateful to be spared the fate of Larkin. Or, surrounded by the hillbillies and the security they offered, switch the blame for this new killing on to the black-clad stranger.

Whichever, Barnaby Gold would take the available appropriate action when the time came. The coin was already spinning. There was no point in trying to predict if it would come down heads or tails.

CHAPTER EIGHT

AFTER he had finished the cheroot, he ate some jerked beef from his saddlebag and drank water from a canteen without stopping and dismounting. He was a half-hour of slow riding away from the clearing and guessed that soon he would reach another hillbilly homestead. Was aware, also, of the possibility that at any moment he was likely to hear Will and Jesse Gershel and however many men they had rounded up coming down the trail.

Three or four hours, the elder Gershel had said, before he and his neighbours would return to the house. It was already more than two since he and his son had left.

The trail and the river had looped away from each other, with a rocky butte intervening. The timber was more sparse in this section of the valley and Gold paid close attention to the way ahead and the terrain to either side. Whatever version of the events at the logger's place the sniper told his neighbours, the men were sure to ride hell for leather to the Gershel homestead. To make sure Martha and the girl were not harmed. And Barnaby Gold wanted to see them before they spotted him in this much more open country.

Then the trail and river converged again and his aim was achieved.

The butte came to an abrupt end at a point where a natural arch of eroded rock spanned the trail. Opposite the end of the butte, a wooded gully cut away and steeply down from the side of the trail. Through the arch, where he reined the gelding to a halt in the afternoon shade of the butte, he was able to look down a gentle slope to the place which was obviously the Bent River Crossing of which Joanne Engel had spoken. The home of the Wolfes, where Virgil and Mary-Ann Engel had visited last night.

The Colorado did curve sharply here, cutting around the base of a sheer, convex escarpment some hundred and fifty feet high on the far side of the river which was sixty feet wide. At the top of the curve there was a break in the cliff with water lapping a few yards into it – beyond which it appeared to become a trail.

Opposite this gap there was another homestead with crop fields to the rear and one side of it. More like the Engel place than that of the Gershels. But smaller. A rowboat and a low-sided ferry craft large enough to carry a wagon and team were moored to the river bank: suggesting the Wolfes did not rely entirely on farming for their income.

But the six riders who emerged from the gap in the cliff had no need of the ferry: they plunged their mounts into the river, unconcerned that the water level in midstream was above their boots in the stirrups. Will and Jesse Gershel were in the forefront of the group – the four men at their backs closer to Will's age than his son's.

These were not the only riders Barnaby Gold could see from the natural arch at the top of the trail that sloped down and ran between the house and the river to continue northward. For eight more were out on this trail, galloping their mounts toward the house: dust from the pumping hooves streaming out behind them. Rising higher into the sunlit air than the spray erupted by the horses in the river.

For a moment, Barnaby Gold thought the reason for the men's frantic haste was that he had been spotted. But, although he was perhaps more than a quarter mile from the house, he realised that this was the objective of both groups of riders. Just a simple frame house with a stoop at the front and shade trees in the yard out back. With a horse hitched to the stoop rail.

A black gelding. Flicking his tail at the flies that were bothering him.

Gold slid from his saddle and murmured: 'Goddamnit it to hell.'

This as the men crossing the river drew rifles and shotguns from their boots.

And a woman ran out of the house. Waving her arms and shouting.

Whatever she was yelling was lost against the splashing of water and thudding of hooves.

The men on the trail drew guns.

Will and Jesse Gershel ran their mounts on to dry land, both of them shouting at the tops of their voices. The other four men came out of the river, flanking the Gershels.

The woman turned suddenly to veer away from the line of galloping animals.

Jesse Gershel exploded a rifle and his father let loose both barrels of the Purdey.

Two more shotguns and rifles showered a hail of death across the screaming, writhing woman toward the front of the house. The horse hitched to the rail reared and snorted.

The six horses with men in the saddles were reined to

dust-billowing halts: this dust clinging to the wet coats of the animals, and the boots and pants of the men who flung themselves from the saddles.

The eight men on the trail slowed to a halt with less fanatical zeal: with the exception of one who leapt from his saddle and raced to crouch beside the hysterically screaming woman.

All guns were back in their boots and holsters now.

The woman was placated and two of the men who had been in the Gershels' group went up on to the stoop of the house. For a moment or so they were beyond Barnaby Gold's range of vision. Then they backed into sight again. In stooped attitudes, each one holding the ankle of a bullet-riddled, blood-trailing corpse.

'Pa, it ain't him!' Jesse Gershel shrieked.

The sniper was face-down when he was dragged to the Gershels. Hatless. Enough of his hair and clothing not splashed by blood to show that both were the wrong colour.

'That's what I was tryin' to tell you!' the woman screamed, wrenching free of the man who helped her to her feet. 'You trigger-happy, crazy fools! He come here to tell you! The man you want got loose from Martha! Killed JL Larkin! Maybe even killed Martha and the girl as well!'

'Frig it, we seen the horse and figured you was runnin' scared from that guy, Gertrude!' one of the sniper's killers yelled.

'You fools never do think anythin' right!' the woman countered. 'Get back on your horses and ride for the Gershel place! See if Martha and the Engel girl have come to harm!'

By the time the men streamed through the natural arch

and galloped their mounts south down the trail, Barnaby Gold and his gelding were concealed in the wooded gully.

CHAPTER NINE

THE woman had been shaken and then hard-slapped out of her hysteria by the man who went to her. Then there had been some more heated exchanges. But low voiced, so that the black-clad man at the top of the slope could not hear what was being said. Part of the talk had seemed to be about whether or not somebody should stay with the woman. But nobody did. A blanket was brought from the house to drape the blood-run corpse where it lay. Then, as Barnaby Gold led his gelding deep into the gully, all the men rode up toward the arch.

Men spanning an age group from twenty to fifty. Most attired in bib aprons over sweat-stained shirts. Homesteaders, all of them. Not expert horsemen and doubtless unused to firing their weapons in rage. Grim-faced and angry. Some looking a little sick at having been involved in the gunning down of the man in front of the Wolfe house. Will and Jesse Gershel almost haggard with anxiety about the fate of a wife and mother.

Ordinary, hard-working men visited by trouble that was snowballing: as decent and honest as most probably, just as John Lloyd Larkin had claimed. Almost in the same breath as he had said he was not prepared to tell the truth unless he was asked.

Then, when they had ridden out of sight beyond the high ground, Barnaby Gold led his horse out of the gully and mounted him: started to ride down the slope away from the arch. A man like few others. Disliking crowds wanting no part of anything at which he did not excel. Totally single-minded in achieving his aims: to the paradoxical extent of allowing himself to be far side-tracked if anything threatened to keep him from his purpose.

He rode toward the house with the sawn-off Murcott unhooked from the rigging ring. The safety catch off and the twin barrels resting across the saddle horn. His approach was heard, but he was not seen until he rode around the corner of the house and along the front.

When the door banged open and the woman who had been hysterical a minute or so earlier stood on the threshold. A tall, thin, gaunt-faced woman of fifty or so. With thinning grey hair, a sallow complexion and a soured mouth-line. Wearing a shapeless grey dress of denim that hung straight from her narrow shoulders to her laced black shoes.

She was holding a heavy, long-barrel Le Mat revolver with a hanging ring in the base of the butt, visible beneath the heels of the two hands in which she gripped it. She tracked his slow progress with the seven inch barrel and then held a rock-steady aim on him when he turned the horse to face her and reined him in.

'Good afternoon, Mrs Wolfe.' He accompanied the greeting with the personable smile.

It did nothing to shift the grimness from her eyes and the set of her mouth.

'You're him, ain't you?'

'You make that *him* sound as if it's in capital letters. As though you were speaking of God.'

'It's the Devil prefers black. And from what I've heard you've done, you could be him. Let that shotgun go.'

'No lady.'

'What?'

'No, lady. Not until you put away that revolver. I don't want to kill anybody, and I don't think you do, either.'

'I could plug you where you sit that horse, young feller!'

'If you're that good with a gun that big, do it, Mrs Wolfe. But if you miss, I'll guarantee I'll have to shovel you into your own grave.'

The woman gasped, stared fixedly into the unblinking green eyes of the man astride the horse: knew it was no idle threat. Then admitted her lack of confidence by allowing the barrel of the Le Mat to sag toward the stoop boarding.

'What do you want here?'

He hooked the shotgun on the rigging ring and swung down from the saddle. Without shifting his gaze from her and with his left hand in the holed pocket of his frock coat.

'Check on the deceased.'

She leaned against the doorframe and now held the revolver one-handed. 'They thought he was you.'

'What I thought, Mrs Wolfe.'

'You saw it.'

He nodded. And turned his back on her to go to where the dead man lay beneath the blanket.

'They saw that black horse of his there and they come runnin'. I come outta the house to tell them it wasn't your horse. But they said they didn't hear me, what with the noise of the water. He must've figured that and he come out to show himself. But they said they was so scared of what might've happened and so mad at you, they just started to fire.'

Gertrude Wolfe gasped again. And let the revolver

clatter to the stoop to put both hands up to her face. Then turned to rush into the house.

Barnaby Gold could hear the wet sounds of her vomiting as, after he had pulled off the blanket, he rolled the corpse on to his back. The exit holes in his back showed he had been hit by two rifle bullets. But the entry wounds at the front were masked by the pepper shot that had ripped through his pants and shirt to tear the flesh from the bones at throat, chest, belly and thighs. His face was not hit – merely splashed with now-congealed blood.

If he had carried anything in his shirt pockets, it had been shredded. One side pocket of his pants was empty. In the other was a comb and thirty-five cents. In his only hip pocket, a five dollar bill and a piece of paper folded into quarter-size.

Gold remained in a crouch beside the body as he unfolded the paper: saw it was a telegraph form with a message scrawled in pencil. But before he could read it he heard a tread on the stoop. Saw Mrs Wolfe was on the threshold again, so draped the shot-shattered body and stood up.

The woman's face had a freshly-washed look. She asked dully: 'You robbin' him?'

'No, lady.'

The telegraph message read: CLINTON DAVIS RIVERSIDE HOTEL BACALL ARIZ LIKELY GOLD STRIKE NEAR YOU SOON STOP ARKIN MISSED GETTING RICH CHANNON EL PASO TEXAS.

He refolded the paper and held it up before putting it into a pocket of his frock coat. Said: 'Just a fair exchange, Mrs Wolfe. I gave him a message. Now I've got his.'

'He asked about you. Before he come back here to the place.'

Barnaby Gold had gone to his horse. Now slid from the

centre of the bedroll, lashed on behind the saddle, three lengths of a pole. One with a triangular shovel piece on an end.

'Anywhere around here you don't want him buried, lady?'

There were short lengths of threaded metal protruding from the ends of two of the poles. He began to screw these into the appropriate receiving holes to form a long-handled shovel.

'Dear God in Heaven, he said you used to be an undertaker,' the woman gasped.

'Nowadays just bury my own dead. Over on the river bank be okay? You're not likely to plough the ground there.'

She made no response and he went to the spot indicated: began to dig into the moist, easy-to-work earth.

'Your dead?'

This after more than a minute. During which time she came down off the stoop and across to where he was digging.

'It might help your menfolk to know he would have died anyway, Mrs Wolfe. Him or me. If I'd known who he was at Larkin's place, I'd have killed him then.'

There was a pause between each sentence in which he shovelled earth from the hole to a heap. He could sense her looking at him intently. Eventually, she said: 'I didn't like him when he first showed up here. Scared me as much as you did. His comin' like you, while my Festus was off the place.'

The erstwhile undertaker practising his former trade said nothing.

'Asked if a man named Barnaby Gold had been along the river. When I told him I'd never heard of you, he described you perfect. Said how you used to be a mortician and still looked like one.'

The grave was being dug quickly, Gold aware that Festus Wolfe might have second thoughts about leaving his wife after Larkin's body was found: come riding back under the arch and down the slope.

'Course, I knew he was talkin' about the very same man Will Gershel said he and Jesse had caught. But even if I hadn't liked the looked of this here feller, I wouldn't have said nothin' about that. Us mountain folk handle our own trouble. So he rode on south without learnin' nothin' from me. And I was like on hot coals waitin' for the men to get back. Tell them about him.'

Gold interrupted his chore, but only to run a coat sleeve across his sweat-beaded face: gave no sign that he was even listening to what the woman was saying.

'But he shows up again first. Without them guns he had before. Says as how he run into you while you was quarrellin' with JL Larkin. How it ended with you shootin' poor old JL who never harmed a fly. Would have shot him, too, he said. Except you wanted him to give a message to the menfolk. Tell them that if any of them stood in your way from leavin' this piece of territory, they'd get the same as JL.'

'Appreciate you telling me all that, lady.'

'Guess it's the truth?'

'No.'

'JL ain't dead?' There was hope in her tone.

'He's dead.'

'Oh.'

'It was an accident.'

'Accident?'

'Clinton Davis was aiming to kill me, but his bullet hit the logger instead.'

'You say? Who's left alive to back your word?' she was immediately afraid at having hurled the challenge. But Gold did not even look up at her. And she moderated her tone to ask: 'Did you have to . . . to . . . hurt Martha and the Engel girl when you escaped?'

'The girl less than she deserved, the woman not at all.'

'We can give thanks to God for that.'

'Okay.'

She began to cast anxious glances up toward the arch of rock.

'I wish you would leave that and go away, young feller.'

Two more shovelsful of dirt were moved from the hole to the heap.

'My Festus and maybe some others could be back any time.'

'Reason I'm working so fast, lady.'

'There'll be shootin' if that happens. And it ain't you I'm worried about. Not after you killed poor Mary-Ann and Virgil just hours since them and me and Festus was laughin' and jokin' in the house here.'

Gold was just three and a half feet down and had come up against solid rock. He climbed out of the grave and saw that Gertrude Wolfe was looking at him quizzically.

'There are two people who can tell I didn't, lady,' he supplied. 'But they've already told it another way.'

Gertrude Wolfe watched as he went to the body, carefully wrapped it in the blanket, hefted it up over his shoulder and brought it back to the graveside. Then he stepped down into the hole and lowered the corpse gently to the earth: face-up inside the makeshift shroud. While she witnessed this, then studied him as he shovelled the dirt back into the grave, there was a pensive expression on her thin, work-wearied face.

Asked: 'When you're through with that, you're goin' to high-tail it away from this stretch of river, young feller?'

'I never high-tail it anywhere, lady.'

'I think you should.'

'So did Mr Larkin.'

'I can believe it wasn't you killed him. That feller you're puttin' in the ground, God rest his soul, I knew he was no good. Didn't know how to talk civil to a lady.'

The body was hidden by dirt now. Gold did not sweat so freely at this easier chore of filling in the grave.

'He had something on his mind.'

'Killin' you.' She paused to invite a comment, but none was forthcoming. 'The whys and wherefores of that ain't got nothin' to do with me and I don't wanna know them.'

It was a lie. Gertrude Wolfe was deeply intrigued by this black-clad, slow-to-talk and totally unruffled young man: calmly burying a stranger on this peaceful riverside which was liable at any moment to explode with renewed violence. Intrigued by him and . . . something else. A mixture of things. Horrified and yet attracted. Admiring his firmness of resolve and at the same time repelled by his callous lack of emotion. She wanted him to be done and be gone; yet felt a strong desire to know why he was as he was. When she could maybe help him to be different. Such a fine looking young man with that blond hair and green eyes. His body so lithe and strong...

The life-wearied and time-lined woman made a sound deep in her throat. Of self-anger. Then felt her sallow complexion become flushed when Barnaby Gold finished his chore and turned toward her: as if she feared he had glimpsed in her expression some clue to her disgusting train of thought.

'Festus and me go to bed early,' she blurted out quickly. 'Sleep deep with clear consciences. We wouldn't hear no one ridin' down the trail in the dead of night. Unless he was makin' a real racket.'

Gold was unscrewing the three pieces of the shovel. 'Appreciate the thought, Mrs Wolfe.'

He started toward his horse to stow the dismantled tool in his bedroll.

'That Joanne Engel's a high and mighty miss for her age. Don't like it that we won't allow marriage before a person is sixteen. Mary-Ann was only talkin' about her last night. About how she was sorry she ever let her know that she was only eleven when she got wed to Virgil back east. Said, too, how she didn't like for the girl to be walkin' out with that no-good Jesse Gershel.'

Barnaby Gold had returned to the edge of the river. To hunker down, wash the dirt from his hands and the sweat from his face.

'But you people didn't leave all the mountain ways behind, lady,' he said as he came erect, wiped his hands dry on his coat and took out a cheroot.

'We take care of our own, sure enough. Deal with our own troubles. But we ain't never had none as big as this before.'

He struck a match on the stock of the Murcott and lit the cheroot before he swung up into the saddle. Saw something akin to sorrow in the dark eyes of the woman. Maybe apology, maybe pity. But in response to his implacable gaze, her feeling turned to anger.

'But you got no call to look so high and mighty about it! Seems to me I never did come across anyone before so set on doin' things his own way! Least we got rules we abide by because they was made for the good of all of us.'

'Sure, Mrs Wolfe. Where there are people, you have to have rules. I'm just one person. Bye-bye.'

CHAPTER TEN

FESTUS Wolfe had brought seven other men down the trail on the Arizona side of the river, but during the remainder of the afternoon, Barnaby Gold rode by only five homesteads. Frame houses and outbuildings amid carefully tended fields of crops.

A dog barked in one of the barns as he approached and went on by. In the house on another property he heard a baby crying. Once, as he rounded an outcrop of rock, he caught sight of a slim woman with auburn hair. She dashed from the house, snatched up a boy of about four playing with a toy handcart and rushed back inside with him. The slamming of the door curtailed the child's tearful protests.

He rode across the front of each river-facing house with the Murcott resting on the saddle horn. Knowing he was being watched from behind windows that glinted in the sunlight. Aware of the possibility that perhaps not every man had responded to Will Gershel's call. Or that a woman, more familiar with guns than Gertrude Wolfe, might be driven to blasting at him by some vivid mental image of wholesale slaughter: conjured up by his appearance on the trail.

But his passing was merely noted. Surreptitiously and

fearfully. And he was followed only by the anxious gazes of the watchers for as long as he remained in their sight. Also, there was no sign of the men who had ridden so hard toward the Gershel homestead in the wake of the bloody killing of Clinton Davis.

Which would have struck most men as odd. But Barnaby Gold gave it no thought. An aroma of cooking food had been mixed in with the smell of woodsmoke curling from the chimney of the last homestead he passed: and thus, after a long period of feeling nothing except for weariness, he began to consider his hunger and how to satisfy it. Decided that the town of Bacall, which could not now be far up the trail, was likely to offer more appetising fare than he carried in his saddlebags. And he smoked another cheroot to help stave off the demands of his stomach for hot food.

The sun sank to a crimson death beyond the ridges of the Chemehuevi Mountains across the river and, when the short-lived dusk had run its course, he saw lights ahead of him. More glints of yellow through blackness than a mere homestead would merit. A mile away from him and more than two hundred feet above. The river curved to the left but the trail continued due north: rising in a series of short grades with lengths of flat between.

The street began at the end of an avenue of pinyons: was even more clearly defined by a lettered board, two wagon widths long and supported on twenty foot high poles to either side. Moonlight illuminated the legend: BACALL WELCOMES ALL.

There was just the one street, rising and curving gently toward the left. The best part of half a mile in length. A hundred feet wide beyond the town marker portal. The buildings to either side isolated on their own broad lots. Most of frame construction. A few of stone and, here and there, one which mixed the two materials.

Houses at the southern end, some of them with fenced property lines. All with shade trees and one with a neatly tended flower garden. Midway along the street, at the top of the curve, were business premises. Stores supplying the basic needs of life, a livery stable, blacksmith's forge, barber shop and a bank. And a funeral parlour to which Barnaby Gold paid no more attention than any other building, as he rode slowly along the centre of the deserted street. All of these darkened and locked up for the night, their hours of business at an end for another day.

Beyond, two more houses on either side of the street. Like those behind the newcomer, three had lights in some windows. One of them had a shingle to proclaim it was a boarding house. Across from this, a doctor advertised his presence.

At one time, this had been the extent of Bacall's northern limit. Although there may have been an older church on the site of the obviously recently built one next to the darkened house. Its neighbour was a meeting hall, then came the stage depot and telegraph office, with the wire stretching northwards from its roof on a line of poles. The Riverside Saloon, named for a narrow creek that cut across the end of the street, was the last building on the left. On the other side, the law office and gaol were next to the boarding house. Then there was a Chinese laundry and the foundations of a new building with a pile of planks nearby.

The creek had a twenty foot long timber bridge with a rail, just wide enough for two people to walk on. But was shallow enough to be forded by wagons and horses. On the far side was another portal, its cross-member doubtless lettered in the same way as that at the southern end of the town.

The only lights on this side of town came from the two-storey frame-built saloon, which looked to be the newest property in town. And it was toward the stooped and balconied façade of this that the black-clad, trail-dusty, travel-weary and hungry Barnaby Gold angled his gelding.

Vented a soft sigh of relief as he got out of the saddle and allowed his horse to drink from a wooden trough before he hitched the reins to the rail. The sounds of the gelding gulping down the water and of the creek rippling past the bridge pilings, the chirping of crickets and the rustling of tree foliage in a gentle breeze were all that disturbed the peace of Bacall.

The batwinged entrance and two windows to either side of this spilled kerosene lamplight across the stoop on which stood two Boston rockers. None of the upstairs rooms were illuminated. And there were no sounds from inside until Barnaby Gold pushed open the batwings and stepped over the threshold.

When a man said: 'Evenin' to you . . . oh, my God!'

It started out friendly and finished on a note of fear.

A woman greeted sensuously: 'Well, hello to you, stranger.'

The saloon was wider than it was deep, with the bar counter running partway along the rear wall: an entertainments platform to the right and a stairway to the left. Fifteen chair-ringed tables took up most of the floor area and there was a circular dance floor with a piano at the side in front of the dais. The walls were white and hung with oil paintings in ornate gilt frames. The ceiling was black with yellow stars and a half-moon painted on it. A dozen lamps hung from the ceiling or wall brackets, but only four of them were lit.

The place smelled of fresh paint and new timber and the furnishings looked virtually unused. A mirror ran along the wall behind the bar, slightly tilted from the top, the section immediately opposite the entrance not fronted by glass and bottle-lined shelves. So that the newcomer had an unobstructed view, in reflection, of his appearance that triggered the two comments.

The battered hat with the narrow brim curled up all around. The frock coat with the two bullet holes in the left pocket. The shirt buttoned to the neck. The pants. The boots. All of them black, powdered with grey dust. Creased, crinkled or scuffed. His face, the lower half heavily bristled while his cheeks and forehead were smeared with dust, ingrained from when he had wiped sweat from the flesh. The gunbelt with several looped bullets in view with the coat open, but the Peacemakers seen only as bulges. The Murcott which he had taken off the rigging ring, gripped in his right, blood-crusted hand, the sawn-off twin barrels pointed at the floor.

He probably looked worse because of the contrast with his surroundings. He felt wearier and dirtier as he crossed the unsullied floor to where the apprehensive bartender stood, dropping motes of dust behind him.

'Hello. Hot food for sale here, sir?'

'We sell everything a man needs in the way of home comforts, stranger.'

This from the woman who sat at a table near the stairway end of the bar. She was as close to thirty as made no difference, with long blonde hair: black roots starting to show. Good-looking, but with a predatory cast to her rounded features. No taller than five feet three inches with an amply curved body that had probably been a little slimmer when she first bought the high-necked, long-sleeved dress she wore. Flame-red with some fancy white trimmings on the bodice, hem and cuffs.

'Food is what the man's hungry for right now, Annie,' the bartender said quickly, struggling to overcome his initial fright at seeing the unsmiling, black-clad, shotgun-toting young man between the batwings. 'Ain't that right?'

'Sure is, sir. Can you do it?'

'No trouble. Annie, go tell the missus, why don't you?'

He was fifty or so. No taller than Annie, who left her game of solitaire to come along the bar. Running her dark brown, heavily made up eyes over the length of Barnaby Gold. Then went through the double doors at the other end of the bar.

'Drink while you're waitin', stranger? Lay the trail dust.'

'Beer would be nice.'

He hurried to draw the drink. A short, rotund man with a circle of black curly hair around his shiny dome. Square-faced and clean-shaven. Hardly any neck. Dressed in a clean white shirt and black bow-tie. With a leather apron tied around his waist.

Gold had leaned the Murcott against the front of the bar and placed a dollar bill on the polished top when the beer was delivered.

'Appreciate it.'

'First one's on the house to any new customer comes in, stranger. On account we've only been open three weeks. Kinda encouragement for folks to call again.'

'Nice of you.' He sank the beer at a swallow and set the empty glass down on the bill. 'Like to pay for another now.'

The house whore re-entered the room while the second beer was being drawn from the pump. 'Mrs Dalton says she hopes meat loaf, beans and sweet potatoes will be okay.'

'Sounds good, lady.'

She sidled seductively along the front of the bar. 'Want to buy me a drink?'

The bartender was in the process of making change from a pocket in the front of his apron. He paused and eyed Gold expectantly.

'No, lady, I don't.'

The seductive pose abruptly switched to one of injured pride. While the bartender hurried to get out the right coins after directing a warning glance at the whore.

Annie bit back on an obscenity and said brittlely: 'Well, you don't have to be so damn rude about it.'

'Was always taught it was rude to ask strangers for anything.'

He sipped his fresh beer.

'I'm Anne Kruger. This is Arnie Dalton. His wife Fran is fixin' your supper. If you tell us your name, we won't be strangers, will we?'

'Barnaby Gold. And I'm still not going to buy you a drink.'

'Leave it, Annie,' Dalton said harshly, eyeing his customer intently.

The whore gave a toss of her head which set her dyed blonde hair swinging. Then overemphasised the sway of her hips when she returned to the game of solitaire.

'Gold, uh?'

'More like iron, as in pig,' Annie rasped venomously.

Dalton tried to mask the words by saying quickly: 'You got no need of that shotgun, Mr Gold.'

'I haven't?'

'The gunsel who was askin' about you – stayed here in the hotel for a week – he left town this mornin'.'

'After he got a telegraph? His name was Clinton Davis?'

A nod.

'He found me.'

Dalton looked tense. Then shrugged his shoulders.

A silence followed, in which Barnaby Gold was the

only one of the trio to seem at ease with it. The bartender and the whore were relieved when the double doors swung open and Fran Dalton emerged. Carrying a tray on which there was a plate of food, mug of coffee and a knife and fork.

She was perhaps ten years younger than her husband. A little taller and much slimmer. Her face was angular and plain, but attractive in the set of her blue eyes and the way her short black hair hugged her cheeks. Somehow sultry. She carried her small-breasted, narrow-hipped body well. Her sexuality far more alluring than the obvious sensualness of the professional seller of favours.

'Here all right, mister?' she asked as she set down the tray on a table at the edge of the dance floor.

'Appreciate it,' Gold acknowledged, aware of the intensity of her glance at him – perhaps indicating that Annie had said more about him than that he was hungry. She went back to the kitchen.

He finished his beer and took the Murcott to the table, laid it on a spare chair. He wiped his hands down his coat before he started to eat. And kept on both the coat and hat. The food was plain, well-cooked and tasty.

Annie continued to play solitaire and Dalton went back to the mail order catalogue he had been reading before Gold entered. But both cast frequent surreptitious glances at the eating man. Apprehensive and riled.

When he had satisfied the edge of his hunger, he asked: 'You have a room I can rent, Mr Dalton?'

'Twelve of them. We're empty right now.'

'Hot bath?'

'No trouble, Mr Gold.'

'The livery is closed. Have a horse outside.'

'Fred Street will be in later. He'll take care of your mount.'

'How about Floyd Polk?'

'The sheriff?'

'Name I was given.'

'The right one. He ain't in town right now. Had to go over to Prescott last week. Due back pretty soon, I guess.'

Another silence, disturbed by the scrape of fork on plate and the swallowing sounds Gold made.

'Bounty hunter!' Annie said suddenly.

Arnie Dalton glared at her.

'Why else would someone like him want to see the sheriff?'

'His business is his own!' He blurted it out so fast that spittle ran down his chin. He wiped it off with his shirt sleeve. 'I've told you before, girl! If you don't watch your mouth, I'll throw you outta this place!'

'I don't kill for money, lady.'

Both of them broke free of the angry stares they were locked on. To gaze at Gold. Who finished the last of his coffee and lifted the Murcott off the chair before getting to his feet.

'Coming, lady?'

'Uh? Where?'

'Upstairs.'

'Well, you've changed your damn tune.'

'Be nice, Annie,' Dalton urged.

'Well,' she said with a petulant pout, but got to her feet. 'He wouldn't even buy me one lousy drink.'

'I'll see Fred Street tends to your mount, Mr Gold.'

'Appreciate it.'

He gestured with the Murcott for Annie to go up the stairs ahead of him.

'When'll you be wantin' to take the hot bath?' Dalton called after him.

The young man on the stairway did not shift his gaze away from the swaying rear of the whore, each movement of the flesh visible because of the tautness of the red fabric stretched over it. He clicked his tongue against the roof of his mouth then called out: 'First things first.'

CHAPTER ELEVEN

'ANY room you like, mister. Mine if you want, but it ain't hardly got space to turn around in.'

The hallway leading off from the head of the stairs was illuminated only by blue moonlight entering through a window at the far end. Gold halted at the first door on the left he came to and swung it open. Went across the threshold into a room with a window overlooking the balcony and the street. Furnished with a double bed with a small table on one side and a chair at the other, a clothes closet, a bureau with a basin and pitcher on it and three small rugs. A kerosene lamp on the bedhead table. Two framed prints of flowers in vases on the wall flanking the bureau.

Annie had to come back down the hallway several yards when she realised he was no longer behind her.

'Don't tell a person what you're gonna do, will you?' she snapped. And slammed the door at her back.

Gold was at the window, and now he opened it a crack at the bottom, after glancing out along the still-deserted street.

'Okay, lady. I'm going to screw you. So get out of those clothes.

'You gonna pull the drapes?'

'No.'

He was at the chair now. Rested the Murcott against it and began to take off his hat and coat.

'So you don't want the lamp lit?'

'I get it cheaper for putting on a show for the local folks?'

Her dress had loops and buttons down the back from the nape of the neck to her waist. She glared her displeasure at him while she put both hands behind her, working at unfastening the loops from the buttons.

He took off his clothing with the same kind of slow deliberation he did most things. Draped each item carefully across the chair. Appeared to pay no attention to the whore as the top of the dress slid off her arms and torso. Nor when she kicked off her shoes, inserted a thumb under the waistline at either side and crouched to push the dress, her underclothing and hose free of her hips and legs. Then stood up and stepped away from the heap of garments on the floor. Totally naked.

Barnaby Gold was still wearing his grey long-johns.

'Most men enjoy watchin' a woman take off her clothes.'

He looked at her blatantly now, as he unfastened the buttons down his chest. 'You're good at it, lady. Fast.'

His eyes, their colour concealed by the darkness, glinted a little in the low level of moonlight as he surveyed her from the ankles up.

Her skin was very white and looked smooth. Her legs were finely shaped: slender, the tapered thighs in proportion with the calves. He had seen the broadness of her hips. Without the camouflage of the flare of the dress's skirt and the constricting influence of the severely gathered waistline, her belly was seen to bulge and there was only a slight inward curve above each hipbone. Her sex was marked with a large and luxuriant triangle of jet black pubic hair. Her breasts were as large as they had promised to be: necessarily drooped into pear-shapes rather than standing as cones. The areas of the nipples were very dark. There was a lot of hair under her armpits.

Since she was a whore, she would not always have been well used by men. Maybe hated all men, if less forthrightly than she loathed Gold. But she had taken care of her body well enough, ensuring that the merchandise she had to sell was attractive to the committed purchaser.

'You like what you see, mister?'

He shrugged out of the top of the long-johns, to reveal a firm fleshed and not overly muscled torso, the matting of hair on his chest fine and as blond as that on his head.

'You hear me complaining, lady?'

'Well, you sure don't look so happy at what you're seein'.'

He straightened up from taking off the long-johns and when the whore raised her gaze from the base of his belly to his face, her mood had altered. From resentful petulance to smiling pride.

'Well, in one way you're as hard as you look, mister.

She brought up her hands to cradle each heavy breast in the palms as she came across the room toward the bed.

'I'll take care of that,' he told her.

She moved around the end of the bed to his side of it and halted a foot in front of him. He reached out and gently caressed her breasts with his hands in the attitudes of claws: his fingertips testing the soft smoothness of her skin while the palms massaged her nipples.

She had dropped her arms to her sides. Now raised them to cup the hard, sparse flesh contouring his hipbones. He moaned softly. Her hands moved around to the back of him and exerted a slight pressure.

'Not yet, lady.'

Footfalls sounded on the street below the cracked open window. Then across the stoop boarding.

'Why don't you call me Anne?'

He made no response. Leaned his head down. She thought he was going to kiss her on the mouth and she pouted her lips in readiness. But instead his face went lower and his hands raised her breasts. He brushed his lips delicately across the upper slope of each.

She leaned the side of her face into his hair. Then, as he continued to move his mouth on her breasts, alternately upon the rough texture of the nipples and the creamy smoothness of the pale skin, she tentatively brought her hands up the sides of his body. To his shoulders, his neck and then his face.

His day's growth of bristles prickled her hands when she clutched his cheeks tightly. But he did not allow her to pull his exploring mouth closer. And his beard did not scrape her flesh. Merely brushed it, to become part of the pleasure his moist lips and tongue gave her.

Now she moaned, and arched her body toward his.

He allowed this to the extent where the hirsute base of her belly made the lightest of contacts with the exposed tip of his sex. And when he held back from her, she moved a hand away from his face: to grasp him.

'Oh, God, it's been so long!' she rasped through teeth clenched in a half-grin, half-scowl of desire.

'Okay, lady,' he said and slowly, in a series of fluid motions, straightened up and eased away from her.

For perhaps a full second, her expression was entirely a scowl: as she released her hold on him and from the utter lack of emotion on his face feared he had merely been toying with her. As a prelude to some kind of punishment for the way she had been toward him down in the saloon.

But then he moved again. To lift her off her feet, turn,

and lay her gently on the bed. And she submitted entirely to him. Forcing herself to control the urgency of her desire as he carefully eased her thighs apart with his clawed hands, knelt on the bed between them and then lowered himself down on to her.

His hands went to her face and held each cheek. His chest hair brushed her nipples. He kissed her on the lips: as gently as every other way he had touched her since she came to him.

She moaned, a sound on the threshold of ecstatic pleasure, as she felt him enter her: experienced, too, the feel of his belly and chest along her body.

For a moment longer, he remained perfectly still: locked into her burning, very wet want to the full extent of his own. Then he raised his lips from her mouth, said: 'Open your eyes, lady.'

She snapped the lids wide and in the soft moonlight from the window her face in its surround of blonde hair on the pillow was a distraught mask: as if she were on the verge of tearful pleading for release. This as he raised himself slightly, still cradling her cheeks in his cupped hands. His own youthful face still totally expressionless.

But then he began to fulfil her searing need. And to ease the pent-up lust he had controlled until now. Withdrawing and thrusting, withdrawing and thrusting. Angling himself into her in such a way that she received the utmost pleasure: driving deeply enough to bring himself toward the peak of sexual gratification at a carefully measured pace.

His eyes held hers in a fixed stare across a gap of twelve inches. His lips stayed in a firm line.

Until she began to roll her head from side to side on the pillow Was allowed to by his hands which continued to hold her. Then she forced her legs wider apart. Writhed her belly and breasts beneath him. Brought up her hands to cup his face. Parted her lips and protruded and withdrew the tip of her tongue between them in a cadence that matched his movements inside her.

Moaned and cried out with soft shrillness. Her eyes closed tightly now. She sweated. Became silent and rigid. Let out her breath, hot on his face, in a long sigh. Felt his lust flood into her. Snapped open her eyes and saw that he was staring at her face in the same way as before. While he spasmed to the climax.

When his features were abruptly softened by a gentle smile.

'Mister, I ain't never had a payin' customer who . . . ' She ran out of breath and had to suck more into her lungs.

'My pleasure, lady,' he told her as he came out of her, released her face and swung off the bed.

He went to the window to look out on the street.

'No one else ever gave a damn about my feelin's.' She sounded surprised to the point of shock. 'Men who use whores, they ain't supposed to.'

There was just one man on the street. Leading the black gelding down the curving slope toward the livery stable. From the saloon below there came a steady buzz of talk, interspersed with a gust of laughter now and then.

'How come, mister?'

'How come what?' He turned from the window and saw that she was still sprawled on the bed, legs splayed and arms outstretched in an attitude of pleasant exhaustion.

'You treated me like dirt down in the saloon. Yet here in this room . . . '

'Appreciate it if you'd go arrange that hot bath for me, lady.'

'Sure. Sure.' She quickly got up from the bed. And he

was stretched out on it before she reached her heap of discarded clothing.

'How much do I owe you?'

'It's two dollars for a short time. You pay Arnie Dalton. If you wanted to give me somethin' extra?'

'No.'

She had put her dress on first and was now getting into her underclothing. 'Damn you!' she flared.

'The liveryman's taken my horse. He should have left the saddlebags. Appreciate it if you'd bring them up.'

'All right!' She pushed her feet into her shoes. Whirled toward the door. But paused with her hand on the knob to look back at him. He still lay flat on his back, naked, hands interlocked at the nape of his neck, gazing up at the ceiling. She spoke softly. 'Will you tell me one thing?'

'It was good.'

'I'm glad.'

'I saw you were.'

'And that was real important to you, wasn't it?'

He clicked his tongue against the roof of his mouth. 'It takes two.'

She sighed ruefully. And shook her head. 'I just don't understand it.'

'Lady, unless you got something other than money out of that screw, it wouldn't have been so good for me.'

'Yes, I know. I don't mean that. I mean I don't understand how you could be the way you was downstairs. Then make love to me like I was the only woman in the world for you.'

'I am what I am.'

'You're like two different people. Hard and mean one minute. Gentle and tender the next.'

He raised his head to look across the room at her. Removed a hand from the back of his neck and held up the forefinger.

'Just the one man, lady. Who only enjoys doing what he's good at. Whores are for screwing. I screwed you and you didn't have any complaint. If I want you again, I'll let you know.'

'Damn you!' She tried to snarl it, but her voice broke and a sob escaped her throat as she wrenched open the door. 'I'd rather go with a thousand men who treat me like the whore I am! Than have you make me feel like a real woman for five minutes! Only to act like I was dirt again before I've . . .'

'Talking of dirt, lady, you want to go arrange for my bath now?'

She slammed the door. Forcefully enough to rattle the window and vibrate the lamp on the bedhead table.

CHAPTER TWELVE

BARNABY Gold was still lying naked on his back on top of the bedcovers, smoking a freshly-lit cheroot, when the door swung open. And a woman gasped.

He raised his head off the pillow and with the cheroot clenched between his teeth, said: 'Mrs Dalton.'

She was carrying a metal hipbath.

'I didn't expect . . . I thought you would be decent.' She had been staring at his nude body. Now averted her head as she carried the tub into the room and set it down. 'I'm sorry, Mr Gold. I should have knocked.'

Anne Kruger came across the threshold behind her, toting two pails of steaming water, with the saddlebags off the gelding draped over a shoulder. A small smile turned up the corners of her mouth while she enjoyed the other woman's discomfiture.

Gold swung his feet to the floor and sat on the edge of the bed. 'It doesn't bother me, Mrs Dalton. But if you haven't seen your husband in this state, you're right. You should have knocked on the door.'

'That is hardly the . . . oh, dear. I'll leave Annie to do the rest.'

She hurried out. And closed the door on the higher volume of noise that came up the stairway from the saloon below.

The whore tossed the saddlebags on the bed, then two towels and a cake of soap from the bath before tipping in the hot water. She was no longer smiling.

'Those men who treat you better than I did, lady?'

'Yes?'

'One of them Jesse Gershel?'

'That hillbilly kid.' She scowled.

'He said he was in this place last night.'

'He had a couple of drinks. He didn't come upstairs with me. Hasn't since the second time. Same as the first. Did it before he touched me almost. Some kids are like that. But that second time, he didn't wanna pay. Blamed me for shootin' off – '

'Just a couple of drinks? Like two?'

'Or three. I didn't keep damn count, mister. Anyway, I was up in Clinton Davis's room some of the time.'

She peered hard at him, seeking a reaction to the name. But there was a knock on the door. Mrs Dalton called that there was more water and to hand out the empty pails. The whore complied and the woman in the hallway kept her head averted again while the door stayed open.

'He wasn't liquored up?'

She had emptied the pails into the bath. The room was getting steamy and there was condensation on the window.

'Not him. Like he can't handle a woman, he's no good with liquor. Got sick to his stomach a few times when he first started to use the place. Just drinks beer now. What's it to you?'

'There were other people in the saloon?'

'Sure. A few.'

'Who saw he was okay when he left?'

'Sure. I guess so.'

'Guess so?'

'Damn it, mister! He wasn't drunk. Just mad.'

'What about?'

'Davis goin' with me, I figure. He stared daggers at us when we went upstairs. The same when we come down later. Muttered somethin' I didn't hear. And Davis laughed at him and said somethin' about him bein' a man some day. Then Jesse upped and went out. Left half a glass of beer. He's just a kid, mister. What's your interest in him?'

Knuckles hit the door again and Fran Dalton called it was the last of the hot water. She was gone from the hallway when the whore went for the buckets. Filled the tub almost to the brim.

'You want me to stay? Scrub your back?'

'No thanks.'

He got up from the bed, tested the heat of the water: lowered himself into it. Some of it slopped over the sides. He clicked his tongue as he began to relish the feel of the water on his sweat and dirt-stale skin.

'You know somethin', mister?' She was at the door, which was still closed.

Gold had sunk down to his neck, the cheroot clenched between his teeth. His eyes were closed and he opened them in tacit invitation for her to go on.

'If you've had some kinda trouble with them mountain people – of which the Gershel kid is one – Sheriff Polk won't be much help to you. They take care of their own problems and Floyd Polk ain't inclined to poke his nose into their business.'

'Bye-bye, lady.'

'What?'

His eyes were closed again.

'Damn you!' The door was jerked open and crashed shut in the same manner as earlier.

Alone, Barnaby Gold bared his teeth in a grin of sheer enjoyment. Remained in the same attitude with the grin on his face until the cheroot was smoked. Then put it out in the water, stood up and soaped himself. Rinsed off the suds and stepped from the tub to towel himself dry. Dressed in all but his frock coat and hat before getting a razor, mug and brush, then squatted beside the tub and shaved his face clean of all bristles.

Men began to leave the saloon. He had not heard any of them come up the stairs with the whore.

He put on his hat and coat, then the gunbelt, and picked up the Murcott. But he did not leave the room. Instead, carried the chair from the bed to the window, used a coat sleeve to wipe it clear of mist before sitting down: the shotgun resting across his knees.

Without exception, the dozen customers he saw leave the saloon and start down the curving slope of the street cast glances up at the window. Which suggested he had been one of the topics of the conversation which had previously reached him as a buzz. He was far enough back from and to the side of the window for them not to see him seated there.

They were the kind of men he had grown used to back in Fairfax and Standing. Business-suited or attired in hard-wearing work clothes. Merchants and professional men, clerks and manual labourers. As hard and tough as their work and lifestyle in a frontier community demanded. Most of them content with their lot which was relatively trouble-free except for the day-to-day problems which beset everybody. With little to talk about outside of small town gossip. Thus, inevitably intrigued – excited by and a little frightened of – the black-clad, heavily armed, uncommunicative young stranger who had ridden into town. Eager to know the reason he was there. But anxious not to be caught in the backwash of any trouble he had brought to Bacall.

Barnaby Gold paid them no heed as, via the crack at

the bottom of the window frame, he heard an occasional snatch of talk: with key words.

'... hillbillies ... Annie ... shotgun ... Gershel kid ... Davis ... gunslinger ... Polk ...'

After they had all gone to their respective homes, the batwings flapped again, and booted feet rapped on the stoopboarding.

'Night, Fred.'

'Be seein' you, Arnie.'

'Sleep well, Mr Street.'

'Oh, Annie, if only I could be sure the wife didn't find out, I could sure sleep well with you.'

'Some day, Mr Street.' Annie laughed.

The liveryman joined her. 'Be the same one pigs can fly, I reckon.'

The final customer stepped off the stoop and staggered a little as he started for home. One wedge of light extending from the saloon was blacked out when the big double doors were folded closed in front of the batwings. Then those from the flanking windows faded and disappeared as the kerosene lamps were doused, two at a time. The voices of Dalton, his wife and the whore were indistinct mutterings for a minute or so. Just one pair of woman's footfalls sounded on the stairway and went along the hall to the far end without pausing outside the room where Barnaby Gold sat. A door was opened and closed. Below, in the rear of the building, another door closed, presumably behind the Daltons in their living quarters.

The man on the chair eased the window open a full inch and struck a match to light a cheroot. Dropped the dead match and then ash on the floor. He regretted not having asked for a pot of coffee to be sent up. But not for long. Wishful thinking about what might have been was as foreign to his nature as daydreaming on what the future could hold.

After the cheroot was smoked, the stub crushed out under a boot heel on the floor, he opened the window another inch. And dozed. Every lamp in Bacall was out by then. And the breeze that had stirred the trees when he dismounted in front of the Riverside Hotel had sprung up again. Was a little stronger now. Rattling the partially-opened window from time to time. He did not go deeply enough to sleep so that he failed to be aware of this noise. Which was the only sound he was aware of until the clop of hooves intruded.

He snapped open his eyes but did not move on the chair. Concentrated on listening to the slow cadence of the hooves on the street. Two horses, being walked up the sloping curve from the south. He listened to their approach for more than two minutes before the animals and their riders were close enough to be within his angle of vision.

Clearly seen in the moonlight which cast their shadows squat and distorted on the street across which eddies of dust occasionally swirled to the dictates of the east wind.

The riders were men not at all like those who lived in Bacall. Nor the mountain people from Tennessee who had moved west. This pair were more like one named Arkin than Clinton Davis.

Tall and well-built, lithe and loose-limbed. Dressed for the trail in spurred riding boots, pants, shirts and Stetsons. With thigh-length topcoats on against the cool night breeze. Not fastened, so that their gunbelts were displayed and they had easy access to the revolvers holstered below their right hips. Their clothing looked to be of good quality and they sat astride expensive saddles with all the accoutrements. On big, strong, well-groomed horses.

Although the shadows from the hat brims hid their faces, Gold got the impression that the two men were well short of middle-age. From the way they sat their saddles, the manner in which the horses were ill at ease with the slow pace and the small amount of trail dust clinging to clothing and horse coats, it looked as if men and animals had taken a long spell of rest not very far south of Bacall.

The newcomers exchanged no words or signals. One taking his cue from the other to angle toward the front of the hotel, coming to a halt beyond Gold's angle of vision. He heard them dismount in unison and step up on to the stoop.

A fist banged on one of the big double doors.

It was at least two hours since the Daltons and the whore had gone to bed. And it required another, longer, louder series of thuds with a fist on the door panel to rouse Arnie Dalton. Who yelled irritably that he was coming. Then muttered in the tone of cursing as he crossed the saloon to the entrance.

He was carrying a lamp which caused waves of light to come and go through the windows. Then two bolts were scraped in their fittings, the doors were opened and a wedge of solid yellowness angled out into the street.

'Do somethin' for you?'

Arnie Dalton sounded apprehensive at the sight of the two strangers.

'Need a drink. Him and me both.'

'Saloon's closed.' A pause. 'What's this?'

'What's it look like?'

'It's ten dollars.'

'What it is. Put it toward your savings for your old age, mister. Go back to bed. Jake and me'll attend to serving ourselves.'

'I don't know about that, gentlemen.'

'Don't plan on getting drunk. After we've had our fill, we'll douse the lamp, close the doors when we leave.'

Just one of the newcomers had taken part in the exchange with Dalton until then. Now Jake spoke: 'We look like thieves?'

'No. I ain't sayin' that . . . '

'Good. If you're scared you got thieves living hereabouts, we'll roust you out of bed to lock the doors after we leave. Thanks.'

Dalton said nothing. Perhaps he had signalled them to enter. Or maybe Jake simply stepped across the threshold, forcing Dalton to back into the saloon ahead of him. Whichever, the lamplight changed shape and moved. The footfalls tracked from the entrance to the bar counter. The doors were closed. The bolts were not shot home. The light from the windows danced and dimmed. Brightened and was still when the lamp was set down on the bartop. Voices were now just small scratches on the silence from below.

Barnaby Gold stood up, leaned the Murcott against the wall and eased the window open to its fullest extent. There was a pained expression on his face as he made each movement: revealing the tension he was experiencing while he strove to do everything in total silence.

The timber of the window creaked a little halfway up the frame, but the sound was no louder than those of the breeze and the creek.

He stepped out on to the balcony and reached back inside for the shotgun. Then, setting down each booted foot with great care, he moved to the corner of the building. And on to the stairway that canted across the side facing the creek. His face did not lose the pained look until he was on the solid ground between the Riverside Hotel and the bank of the water course.

The breeze stirred his open frock coat as he started

back along the side of the building, then turned to go across half the front. The horses hitched to the rail looked at him fleetingly. Lost interest in him. The street, with small puffs of wind-stirred dust dancing on it, was otherwise empty.

He did not have to go up on to the stoop to see into the saloon through the window to the right of the entrance: had the height to see as much as he needed while standing on the street.

The two newcomers were standing at the bar, their broad backs to him. Each had a shot glass in his hand. Arnie Dalton, dressed in a blue nightshirt, was starting toward the double doors that gave on to the kitchen and, presumably, the private quarters of the hotel. He glanced back at his late night customers twice. And both times it was plain to see the dread that was deeply inscribed on his pale face.

'Night to you, Mr Dalton!' This from the one who had done most of the talking when they arrived.

Dalton opened and closed his mouth twice. Only then managed to call out: 'Good night, gentlemen!'

'Thanks for your trouble!' Jake added.

Then the hotelman went through the double doors. And the dialogue section of the play in which Dalton had taken such a reluctant role was over. Then one of the men still on stage finished his rye, crouched out of sight of Gold for several seconds. Straightened again to put his boots on the bartop. Jake nodded to him and the man drew his revolver and took long, silent strides toward the foot of the stairway.

'This sure does taste good, Chester! Near as good as that first bottle of liquor we had after we got to Dodge City that time! You recall that, partner? Hell, we swallowed some dust that trip, didn't we? That sonofabitch of a trail boss had us riding drag the whole . . .'

Chester had moved outside Barnaby Gold's range of vision now. Jake poured two more shots from the bottle, but did not lift either glass. For to drink would have left a gap in the monologue he was addressing to himself in the mirror on the wall behind the bar. His reflection showed him to be an ugly man of a little over thirty. Hard-eyed and with a bushy black moustache, teeth of almost the same colour, and a knife scar on his right cheek.

As he continued to recall the events on the trail drive and its rewards in Dodge City, Kansas – not pausing to allow his absent partner an opportunity to interject – his tone altered to take account of whether the memories were pleasant or painful. But his expression of tense expectancy did not change at all.

'. . . whole time! But the grub was real fine, wasn't it? What was the cook's name? Joe Maguire, wasn't it? Got roaring drunk with that big red-headed whore and chased her stark naked out of the room! Man, did she have the biggest . . .'

On the upper floor a door crashed open with a kick.

Chester snarled: 'You've had it, undertaker!'

Barnaby Gold clicked his tongue against the roof of his mouth. And drew the wood-butted Colt from its holster.

A revolver was fired, the bullets exploding from the muzzle so fast the man had to be fanning the hammer.

Jake's image in the mirror abruptly showed a blackened-toothed grin of pleasure. And he raised one of the glasses of rye toward his mouth.

The horses made nervous sounds and movements at the sudden burst of rapid fire gunshots.

Gold thumbed back the hammer of his Peacemaker and took a double-handed grip on the butt. Pressed his elbows against his chest with the Murcott cradled across them. Aligned the barrel of the Colt on Jake's broad back.

'Shit!' Chester shrieked as the gunfire was curtailed. The tone was almost maniacal. 'Jake, he ain't here!'

Jake hurled away the glass and whirled. His left hand streaking to his holstered revolver.

Gold squeezed his trigger. The bullet shattered the window to send a spray of shards across tables, chairs and the floor. Drove into Jake's chest. Too high. The impact slammed him against the bar counter, but he completed his draw. Fired from the hip.

Yelled: 'On the street!'

His bullet took out a triangular fragment of glass still held in the window frame. Then thudded into a balcony support.

Gold exploded a second shot from the Peacemaker. This as Jake dropped into a crouch. Which placed his head in the line of fire. The bullet smashed through his discoloured teeth set in a snarl of rage. Banged the back of his head against the front of the bar counter. Blood erupted from his mouth and he collapsed out of Gold's sight.

Light spilled from the houses down the curving street. Questions were shouted. The two horses snorted and reared, trying to jerk free of the hitching rail.

Against the noise, Gold holstered the Colt and swung up and over the stoop rail, thumbing off the shotgun's safety catch. Dropped into one of the rocking chairs that was immediately below the point where the window of his room looked out on to the balcony and street.

The horses became calm. Questions to which there had been no positive answers were still being asked. But not so loudly now that the silence after the gunfire lengthened.

In the private quarters at the rear of the hotel, Fran Dalton was crying in fear. Her husband was rasping at her to be quiet.

The breeze stirred the leaves of the trees. The creek made rippling sounds beneath the bridge.

No one emerged from the houses. The citizens of Bacall anxious to know what had happened, but all of them too afraid to be the first to investigate the cause and result, until somebody guaranteed it was safe to do so.

Barnaby Gold wore the pained expression again as he strained to hear any sound that Chester might make. His left hand was fisted around the twin barrels of the shotgun and his right index finger was curled across the front of both triggers. His elbows rested on the arms of the rocker and the Murcott was angled across his chest. Behind his pursed lips, his tongue was poised to click.

He heard an intake of breath above him. This a moment after Arnie Dalton had silenced his wife with a slap.

There was no sound of Chester's unbooted feet stepping out on to the balcony. But a few motes of dust floated down from a crack between two planks.

Gold shifted his elbows off the chair arms and held the Murcott vertically, squeezing the base of the stock between his thighs. A line of sweat beaded his upper lip as he stared up at the darkness of the underside of the balcony.

There was neither sound nor sign that the man had swung his trailing legs out over the window-ledge.

From the second-storey hallway, Annie Kruger called softly: 'Barnaby?'

And this caused Chester to catch his breath in surprise.

Gold tracked the gun and his eyes toward the front of the balcony: and had to rock the chair back a little to draw a bead on the point from above which the small sound had come.

He squeezed both triggers.

The horses snorted and reared again in response to the

massive sound of the two barrels being discharged: the belch of flame and smoke from the muzzles. And one of them jerked loose, wheeled and bolted away, its hooves beating on the planking of the bridge. Before it lost his footing and stumbled into the creek. Recovered, and galloped out along the north trail.

Something fell heavily from above, thudding to the ground through the billowing dust of one horse at the gallop and another still rearing on its tether.

Chester. Still alive, for the planks of the balcony had absorbed most of the power of the shotgun's double blast. And it was probable that pieces of shredded timber torn out of the balcony floor had done as much damage to the man as the Murcott's twin loads. He lay on his back in the settling dust, his thighs and belly and face sheened with crimson. A portion of his intestines hung out through a hole in his flesh. He made moaning sounds and blood bubbled in his mouth. His hands kept clenching and unclenching, as if he imagined there was some physical hold with which he could cling on to life.

Barnaby Gold got quickly up from the rocker, holding the shotgun low down at his side. Went to the gap in the balcony rail and drew the Peacemaker from the holster.

'They . . . said . . . you . . . was . . . just . . . a . . . frigging . . . kid.'

'Growing up fast, mister.' He aimed the Peacemaker at Chester's blood-covered face and stooped so that the muzzle was just an inch from the pain-creased brow. Squeezed the trigger.

The hole drilled into his skull looked insignificant compared with the gory injuries that the shotgun blast had caused. He twitched once and was still.

Up on the balcony, the whore gasped. And accused in a shocked tone: 'My God, he wasn't a horse. The sawbones could maybe have saved his life.'

Barnaby Gold glanced up at her as he slid the gun back in the holster.

'Lady, he tried to kill me.'

He said nothing else before turning to go up on to the stoop.

CHAPTER THIRTEEN

THE breeze outside quickly neutralised the acrid stench of gunsmoke. But within the confines of the saloon the exploded powder of Jake's two shots still clung to the atmosphere. This as Barnaby Gold crossed to the bar counter and leaned over the heap of the gunman's corpse to pick up a sheet of paper from beside the still-filled shot glass. The stub of a pencil lay nearby.

While he was reading what was scrawled on the paper, he heard the doors from the kitchen open. And the whore's tread on the stairs.

Barnaby Gold staying here? one of the gunslingers had written. Then, on another line: *Write yes or no or we'll kill you first.*

Dalton's hand was trembling with fear, so that the *Yes* he wrote was barely decipherable.

Keep talking. Which room?

Ferst left top of stars.

Chester had known what the terrified Dalton meant.

Give answers. Go to bed.

'You can see they made me,' Dalton said fearfully after Gold put the paper back on the bar. 'Not only me. I was afraid for Fran, too. And Annie.'

Gold folded the paper neatly and put it with the telegraph he had taken off the corpse of Clinton Davis.

'It's all right, Mr Dalton. I've got no quarrel with you.'

'What was their quarrel with you?' Fran asked.

She had draped a large coat over her nightdress and was clutching it together across her sparse breasts. Her eyes were red from weeping. There was the beginning of a dark bruise on her left cheek where Arnie had hit her into silence.

'It's not our business,' her husband said quickly.

Running footfalls sounded out on the street.

'Somethin' to do with them mountain folks, I'll bet,' the whore muttered. If she used a nightdress in her trade, it was not the one she wore now, which was of unappealing red flannel, draping her full body shapelessly.

There were gasps of shock and some strangled curses as the citizens of Bacall came close enough to see what was left of Chester.

Then: 'Arnie? You and Fran okay? What happened here?'

'Nobody gives a shit about me!' Annie Kruger snarled. And turned to go back upstairs.

Gold took the same route.

'I'll have our mortician take care of the bodies,' Dalton called.

'Nobody will touch them except me.' Gold's voice was soft, but insistent, as some faces showed above the batwings. 'Appreciate it if you'd have Mr Street open up his livery so I can get what I need.'

'You're leavin'?' He sounded surprised, and ready to be pleased.

'Not right now.'

The whore was halfway along the hallway to her room. When he reached the top of the stairs, she asked: 'You want me again?'

'Seeing a man get killed make you want a live one, lady?'

'Damn you, I was worried about you! After the shootin' started.'

She swung around and hurried to reach her room. Again slammed the door. By which time Gold was in his room. He went to his saddlebags and took out two cartridges for the Murcott and three for the Colt. Reloaded both weapons and went back downstairs.

Fran Dalton was gone. Her husband was behind his bar, pouring drinks for the five men – coats on over their nightshirts and boots unlaced – who had run to the scene of the violence. All of them looked at the black-clad, shotgun-toting young man with apprehension.

'Fred Street's gone to open his place like you said, Mr Gold,' Dalton said.

'Them hillbillies wouldn't've hired no gunslingers to do their dirty work, mister,' a tall, gaunt-faced, bespectacled man added. Then, after Gold had given a nod of acknowledgement to Dalton and stooped to grab hold of the back of Jake's coat collar: 'I run the funeral parlour here in Bacall.'

'I'm like the mountain people, sir. Do my own dirty work.' He dragged his limp burden to the batwings, then paused to ask: 'Any particular part of the cemetery you want me to bury them?'

An elderly man, short and pot-bellied, with a white beard, growled: 'We don't want filth like that buried in our churchyard.'

'Fine.'

'In our town even.'

This as the batwings flapped.

The street was deserted again, but with more lights on now. With the Murcott in the crook of an arm, Barnaby Gold got a grip on Chester with his free hand. Then began to move backwards in a crouch. Dragging both corpses to the end of the street, then across the shallow creek. The water came up to his knees. He left the remains at the side of the trail beyond the town marker and recrossed the creek.

Walking past the entrance to the saloon, he heard Arnie Dalton say: '. . . just before he started blastin' into the empty room. He called that Gold feller an undertaker. And then . . . '

The middle-aged, powerfully-built, square-faced liveryman was still hungover from the drinks he had taken in the saloon. He was sitting on a wooden crate, cradling his head in his hands, when Gold entered – and saw that the horses of Jake and Chester were enstalled there.

'You want your mount, mister?'

'No, sir. Just something from my bedroll.'

There was no lamplight in the stable, but enough from the moon came in for Gold to see his way to the corner Street indicated, where his saddle and bedroll hung from a wall hook.

'Appreciate you taking the trouble to open up for me, Mr Street.'

He carried the three pieces of the shovel outside. The liveryman followed him through the doorway and snapped the padlock closed.

'Trouble? I don't reckon I know the meanin' of that word, mister.'

Then, despite his pounding head, watched in fascination as the younger man screwed the three pieces of the shovel together.

'Bye-bye,' Gold said when the chore was done. And turned with the Murcott in one hand and the shovel in the other to go back up the sloping curve of the street.

'What? Oh, yeah. Night to you, mister.'

Other eyes watched him out of sight. Then the men in

the saloon surveyed him curiously as he went back over the creek. Until lighted windows began to darken. The group in the Riverside Saloon broke up and headed again for home. Casting backward glances toward Barnaby Gold who worked slowly and deliberately at digging a two-man grave beside the trail on the far side of the creek.

Soon, just a single lamp in the saloon augmented the moonlight. And only the rhythmic thud of the shovel into dirt provided sound in addition to those of the breeze and the running water.

Gold's mind was empty of thoughts as he worked on the grave with the apparent ease that came with long experience.

First Arkin, then Davis. Now Jake and Chester, whose surnames he did not know. He had been warned that to anger the Channons of Texas was to invite the attention of every gunslinger greedy for a share of the family's wealth.

What was the point of regretting the series of events that had caused him to give the Channons a thirst for vengeance? There was no way to alter the past. Just as pointless to wonder how many more like these he would have to bury. Before the Channons called a halt. Or, more likely, got off the first and decisive shot.

And this was undoubtedly the most likely ending the future held. Because the four men he had been forced to gun down on account of the Channon family's reputation had all made the mistake of underestimating Barnaby Gold.

Arkin had known nothing of the young man except that he was a small town undertaker.

Clinton Davis had known that Arkin had failed – perhaps assumed he was dead – but was unaware of the details.

To Jake and Chester, he was *just a frigging kid.*

But as the death toll mounted and the knowledge of it spread, the other hired guns who were out there in the darkness, even now hunting for him, would not be so easy to beat to the killing shot. They would be much more wary in approaching this blond-haired, green-eyed, good-looking young man who had already buried four of their kind.

Then there was the prospect of ending his trouble with the mountain people along the Colorado south of Bacall. The possibility that they had held off so far because of some deal that was reached with Jake and Chester . . .

Barnaby Gold might have considered some or all of these points while he dug the six foot deep grave, laid the two men face-up in the bottom and then refilled it. But he did not give a thought to any of them.

And only the fact that the Murcott was never out of arm's reach as he was working indicated that he was aware of being in mortal danger that could strike at any time.

When he was finished, heaping the dirt into a neat mound along the length of the grave, he lit a cheroot and dismantled the shovel. His boots and pants were dry now and he used the footbridge to cross the creek.

In the saloon he closed and bolted the entrance doors, and doused the lamp before he went up to his room: noticing that Dalton had failed to wash up the dirty glasses from the late night drinking session, and neither had he swept up the shards from the bullet-shattered window.

Up in his room, in the moonlight, he saw there were five bullet holes in the bedcovers and mattress beneath. So there had been one shell left in Chester's six-shooter when he climbed out on to the balcony to search for the man missing from the bed. He had died in pain and disappointment after confidence replaced anger and fear.

Gold laid the Murcott, his gunbelt and the dismantled shovel on the chair. Then undressed to the extent of removing his hat, frock coat and boots before he got under the bedcovers. The window remained fully opened, but no sounds loud enough to disturb his rest intruded into the room.

Instead, it was a woman.

CHAPTER FOURTEEN

HE did not hear the tentative knocking on the door, nor the gentle opening and closing of it. Followed by the padding of bare feet to the side of the bed. Her regular breathing as she stood in the moonlit, night-cooled room looking down at his head on the pillow for several seconds.

Then, very softly: 'Barnaby. Barnaby Gold.'

He was sleeping the sleep of the contented. And she had to reach out a nervous hand, to touch his shoulder then call his given name again before his eyes snapped open. He blinked several times, disorientated in the first moments of waking. Not recognising her because she had her back to the window.

'It's me, Francis Dalton.'

'Goddamnit to hell,' he murmured, and pulled himself up into a sitting posture, his back resting against the head of the bed. He fisted the grit of sleep from his eyes. 'Something wrong, Mrs Dalton?'

She shook her head. 'No. Nothing. I'm sorry to disturb you.'

'Then why did you, lady?'

She was dressed in the same way as when he had last seen her in the immediate aftermath of the killings. With a long, dark coat draped over her shoulders. Clutching it together at her breasts, the lower front veed open to reveal a white nightgown. But her head-hugging, short hair was no longer dishevelled from sleeping. She had brushed it and it had a sheen in the moonlight.

She drew erect and tense at his curt, flatly-put query. Blurted softly: 'I meant there's nothing wrong for you, Barnaby. But me, I . . . I need help.'

He reached into his coat, draped over the chair to get the box of cheroots and matches. He lit one and on a stream of smoke asked: 'Help?'

'You'll be leaving town tomorrow?'

'If that's when Sheriff Polk comes back, Mrs Dalton.'

'He's expected.'

'Okay.'

'So it has to be tonight.'

'It does?'

'Oh God, yes.'

'What?'

'Make love to me, Barnaby.'

She had been gazing directly into his face. But now she dropped her head to stare at both her hands clutching at the front of her coat.

'You want to pinch me, Mrs Dalton.'

'What?' She continued to hold the attitude of shame.

'If I'm not dreaming this, that'll be less painful than testing it with the lighted end of this cheroot.'

Now she forced her head half-up, to stare at his face with the tops of her eyes. There was a greater tension in her voice.

'Annie told me how it was with you. She tells me how it is with any new man who pays to use her. Oh, God, this sounds awful. But you have to understand. Arnie's a fine husband in so many ways. But when we're in bed, he's . . . he's so totally selfish.'

She shook her head. 'No, it may not be like that. He

can't help himself, perhaps. It's over so quickly for him.'

'I don't want to hear this, lady.'

'Please, just so you'll understand. At first, when we were married, I always told him it was good for me. I thought he'd get better. Make it so that I could get – '

'I can't help you, Mrs Dalton.' His green eyes glinted in the moonlight and his tone was far colder than the night air entering through the same open window.

'Just so I can know what it's like,' she blurted. 'Just the once in my life. In a town like this there's no chance for me to . . . with any of the men who live here.'

'Best you leave this room now.'

'I've never before. Not once with any of those other men Annie told me about. But when I first saw you downstairs . . . when I brought you your meal . . . you struck something inside me, Barnaby. Then when she told me. Said how you treated her up here. Her a whore.'

His eyes were accustomed to the low level of light now. He saw her pale face in the frame of jet black hair: knew that her dark eyes which were spilling tears down her cheeks would be expressing the same mixture of desperate pleading that sounded in her whispering voice.

'I'll give you two choices, Mrs Dalton.'

He sucked on the cheroot and in the red glow of the burning tobacco glimpsed the sudden eagerness, on the brink of high excitement, with which she looked at him.

'Yes?'

'You can go to the door, open it, go through it and close it behind you. Or I can open and close it for you. And in between, toss you through by the scruff of your neck.'

A sob escaped her throat. He drew hard against the cheroot again and in this period of brighter light he saw she looked on the verge of venting a string of curses at him.

But then she whirled around and went to the door. Instead of opening it though, she halted, jerked the coat off her shoulders and dropped it to the floor. Then with a fast, fluid movement, pulled the nightgown up over her head, dropped it on top of the coat and turned to face the watching man on the bed.

Her naked body was a match for her face. Lean and angular, a world removed from the full-blown, obvious sexuality of Anne Kruger's looks and figure. Slim-waisted and narrow-hipped, the belly flat and the thighs slender. The small breasts were firmly conical even while she was standing, her back pressed to the door. The area of the nipples small in the diameter of their darkness but large to the extent of her readiness to be taken. Just as the triangular marking of her sex was almost diminutive, but very bushy.

'Annie has more of everything,' she said softly after allowing a silence during which Barnaby Gold surveyed her nakedness. 'But she's been used so many times. Only one man has had me, and all he's ever done is prepare me for . . .'

She let her voice trail away, and her look of challenge was replaced by one of breathless expectancy while she watched him slowly turn back the bedcovers and swing his feet to the floor. Stand up and crush out the cheroot on the wall. Check that all the sparks were out before he started to come toward her.

Then she held out her arms to him, her lips parted and she ran the tip of her tongue along between her teeth.

'I promise you, you won't be sorry, Barnaby.' She closed her eyes and vented a soft sigh as he moved between her outstretched arms.

'Okay, Mrs Dalton.'

'Fran.'

She interlocked her fingers at the nape of his neck. And

her flesh trembled when he stooped to hook one arm behind her knees as the other went around her back. Then she moaned and pushed her face into the crook of his neck when he lifted her smoothly and easily off her feet.

'Treat me like the woman I know I am, Barnaby,' she whispered, her warm breath on his ear. 'Make me feel the way a woman is supposed to when she gives herself to a man.'

He started to carry her toward the bed.

'Oh, how I've longed for a moment like this, my darling.'

He stopped and leaned forward slightly.

'You have to let go from around my neck now, lady.'

'Oh, yes. Anything. I'll do anything you ask me to, Barnaby.'

She freed her hold on him. And he let her go. It was too far to fall. She started a gasp of alarmed surprise. Then vented a short scream as her naked flesh hit the night-cooled, scummy water in the hipbath. The sound short-lived, because the coldness of the water took her breath away.

Barnaby Gold came erect after holding down his hand to keep the back of her head from banging against the rim of the tub.

'You evil monster!' she rasped at him.

After staring up at him in rage: venting her anger in a whisper when she saw his warning finger pressed to his lips. Then she struggled to get out of the water, but he dropped on to his haunches and held her down with a hand under the surface, splayed on her belly.

'I am what I am, lady.'

She bit back on a snarling retort. Asked simply: 'Why?'

'It's the way I'm made.'

She shook her head. 'Why did you do this to me?' Anger got the better of puzzlement. 'You're nothing like the man Annie thinks you are. Can't you handle two women in one night?'

'Not when one of them's married, lady.'

'That's no damn excuse.'

He nodded. 'Not an excuse. A reason.' He stood up. 'Best you dry off now and go back to your husband. If he wants anything, guess you'll be glad it'll be over fast.'

He went to the bed and sat on it. Watched her while she got from the tub, towelled herself vigorously and put on her sparse clothing. Bitter resentment was inscribed deeply into the flesh of her face and showed in her every move. Then, when she was ready to leave, a different brand of pleading was directed toward Barnaby Gold.

'You won't mention this to Arnie?'

'Best for him if he never knows. Or only finds out after you're dead, Mrs Dalton.'

She looked hard at him, trying to read what lay behind his deadpan expression and flat tone. Then said suddenly: 'You were married. And she cheated on you.'

'Just go, Mrs Dalton.'

She opened the door. 'And she's the reason you are what you are.'

He clicked his tongue against the roof of his mouth. 'No, lady. She's the reason why I have to kill some men before I can be what I want to be.'

'What's that?'

'In Europe.'

She seemed about to ask another question. But from the way he sat on the edge of the bed, peering across the room and out through the window, his profile hard-set, she decided against it. Was about to close the door on him.

'Mrs Dalton?'

'Yes?'

'Do something for me?'

'Why the hell should I?'

'Part of the service here.'

'What?'

'Go get the whore and send her to me.'

'Whoring won't get you over losing a woman you loved as much as your wife.'

'It'll ease the feeling I've got from seeing and holding you stark naked, lady.'

CHAPTER FIFTEEN

SHERIFF Floyd Polk was a big man in build. Three inches taller than six feet and weighing close to two hundred and fifty pounds. He was in his mid-forties and maturely good-looking with liquid brown eyes and a full and generous mouth: his lined and tanned complexion emphasised by a full head of slicked down, whitening hair that showed just an occasional strand of black.

He was dressed in blue denim pants, a brown shirt with white piping on it, red kerchief with white polka dots and a brown Stetson. Despite the trail dust clinging to his outfit, the clothing looked newly purchased. As did the gunbelt with an etched Remington .44 in the right hip holster.

The pinto gelding he rode and the saddle he rode in were past their prime, but well cared for.

Barnaby Gold watched Bacall's lawman ride down the north trail a little after sunrise: standing at the open window in the process of getting dressed while Anne Kruger continued to sleep soundly in the bullet-holed bed, her naked body covered by blankets.

The lone rider, who looked pleasantly weary from a long but not arduous trip, did a double-take at the mound of the fresh grave before fording the creek. Then briefly surveyed the saloon's shattered window: but gave no indication that he was aware of being watched from above as he moved on by, down the deserted curve of the street, the five-pointed bright metal star pinned to his left breast pocket glinting in the early sunlight.

He dismounted just beyond the church and went from sight between it and the house next door.

Gold finished dressing and then went out through the window, along the balcony and down the stairs at the creek side of the hotel, wearing his gunbelt but leaving the Murcott in the room. By the time he was seated in the rocker from which he had fired the shotgun a few hours earlier, the sheriff had opened the front door and two windows to rid his house of the stuffiness from being empty for a lengthy period. Gold lit his first cheroot of the day and waited patiently as smoke began to wisp from the house chimney.

It was perhaps fifteen minutes before Polk reappeared on the street, his clothing brushed free of dust and carrying a large mug of steaming coffee. To cross diagonally toward the law office and gaolhouse.

Gold set out on a converging course and Polk was turning a key in the lock of the door when his caller reached him.

'You opening up for business, Sheriff Polk?'

'My job lasts twenty-four hours in a day if it's necessary, son. Leave the door open, will you.'

The office was small and functional. A desk with a comfortable chair in back of it and a hard-seated, straight-backed one in front. A small table with a free-standing closet next to it against one wall. A rifle rack with six Winchesters padlocked in place across from this. A one-piece metal door with a spy-hole in it which gave on to the gaol section of the building. No clutter and just a thin coating of dust on everything, this having gained entry along with the stuffy air via ill-fitting windows and the crack around the door.

Polk set down his mug on the desk, dropped loose-limbed into the chair behind it and indicated his visitor should take the other one in front. Then he began to sip his coffee noisily, eyeing Gold expectantly over the rim of the mug. Until he noticed the ash on Gold's cheroot was growing long. When he drew open a drawer, took out a burn-stained tin can lid and pushed it across the desk.

'Appreciate it.'

'No trouble, son. Way I like it to be in this town.'

'How far does your jurisdiction extend, sheriff?'

From another drawer, he took out a large sheet of paper, folded several times. Gave Gold the chore of unfolding it. To see it was a three foot by four foot map of the area around Bacall. With a heavy red pencil line marking the boundaries of Polk's authority. A strip of terrain much longer than it was broad, limited to the west by the Colorado, the high points of the Mohave Mountains to the east and the Bacall Creek to the north. His domain spread far enough southward to encompass all the homesteads worked by the mountain people from Tennessee.

Gold refolded the map and pushed it back across the desk. 'There was a lot of trouble during yesterday and last night.'

A nod. 'It goes with your kind, son.'

'My kind?'

'Don't play the innocent with me. The ordinary man doesn't wear the kind of rig you got slung around your middle, son.'

'I came here to tell you about the trouble, sheriff.'

'I'm listening.'

Barnaby Gold told him. Giving him an even-voiced catalogue of the killings since he discovered the carelessly buried corpses of Virgil and Mary-Ann Engel.

When Polk had finished his coffee and did not have the big mug to hide behind, his face was seen to be as impassive as that of the black-clad young man he was listening to.

Then: 'This Clinton Davis and the two men you buried on the far side of the creek? Just personal, you say. So as lawmen hereabouts I can just forget them three are dead and in the ground.'

Gold clicked his tongue and crushed out what remained of his cheroot in the lid. 'Pro gunslingers, sheriff. Hired by a family in west Texas called the Channons. To find me and kill me. There'll be more. Which is why I want this trouble with the homesteaders cleared up.'

'Reckon I can understand that. But first I'll need to be sure about the three men you buried, son.'

'Okay.'

'Can't just take your word about the way they died. Talk to the Daltons and Annie about the shoot-out at the hotel. Then take a ride down to the Wolfe place. Because if you didn't shoot down two men in self-defence and that Clinton Davis didn't die the way you told it . . . ' He shrugged his broad, expensively clothed shoulders. 'Well, son, I'll be forced to conclude you lied about the rest of it.'

The two men gazed into each other's eyes fixedly.

'You get my drift, son?'

'When you can't sweep trouble under the carpet, you sell it down the river, Sheriff?'

Another shrug. 'A man can only be hanged once. And it seems to me, it don't matter who does the lousy job.'

Gold got to his feet. 'Appreciate you being such a good listener, sheriff.'

'Make one stipulation, though.'

'Uh?'

'I need to be sure the man is guilty of a hanging crime.'

Gold nodded and turned to leave the office.

'Son?'

The younger man halted on the threshold and looked back over his shoulder.

'You best remain in town until I've completed my investigation. Because if you don't I may have to consider flight as an admission of guilt. And even if I or the hillbillies don't catch up with you, some sheriff or bounty hunter will. After I've telegraphed a wanted flyer on you. All right?'

'All right.'

Barnaby Gold stepped out on to the sun-bright street and smelled the woodsmoke from many chimneys in the warm air.

He turned to walk down the curving slope, heading for the commercial section of Bacall, his good-looking face offering no clue to how he felt about the attitude of Sheriff Floyd Polk.

It was still very early and none of the stores were open so he went on by. And the aromas of cooking food and bubbling coffee began to permeate the smoke-tainted atmosphere as he took his lone walk to the southern end of the street.

Moving between the tree-shaded houses with their picket-fenced gardens in this section of town, he sensed eyes watching his progress. And paid them no heed.

He crossed the town limit under the overhead sign and came to a halt. Stood for several minutes gazing implacably out along the trail that snaked down the high ground into the valley, where lived a group of people who took care of their own trouble.

No homestead was close enough to be seen from this viewpoint. And there was no sign that the men who worked the homesteads were riding toward Bacall. To ensure, perhaps, that the gunslingers hired by the Channons of Texas had for once relieved the Gershels and the Wolfes and the rest of the need to utilise vigilante justice.

Ride for Bacall they certainly would. Unless Sheriff Floyd Polk was better at his trade than Jake and Chester, Clinton Davis and Arkin had been.

Barnaby Gold moved off the trail to the side of a small wood. Selected a lightning-struck oak some twenty feet away, drew the Peacemaker from the holster and emptied its chambers into the charred and dead tree. Gripping the gun double-handed and holding it out at arm's length, at eye level.

The burst of gunfire erupted shouts of alarm from the houses at the southern end of the street.

He glanced briefly and indifferently at the men and women who came from doorways to see the reason for the shooting. Then closed to within ten feet of the oak and began to practise with the swivel-rigged Peacemaker. Spacing the shots at three-second intervals.

He could absorb the recoil much better now. And the groupings of the bullet holes had improved greatly.

The eagle-butted Colt .45 was fully reloaded and he was ejecting the spent shells from the holster gun when Polk rode his gelding under the town sign.

'Arnie Dalton told me about the piece of paper you got, son,' the lawman called. 'And Fran and the whore back up the town shootings were self-defence.'

'Okay.' Gold began to push fresh shells into the chambers of the revolver.

Polk reined his mount to a halt on the trail. 'From what they said and the damage I saw at the hotel, you don't need the target practise, son.'

'Guess you don't have the ambition to be the best lawman in the country, sheriff?'

He nodded. 'That's right. But then my life doesn't depend on being it. One thing.'

'Uh?'

'You've killed your last man on my territory. So don't you go blasting at anything except trees around here. I'm not, nor ever will be, the best lawman in the country. But I take pride in being as good as I can be.'

'If more Channon guns ride in, sheriff?'

'Lie low. I'll take care of them.'

'And if the Gershels talk you around to their way of thinking?'

'I'll hold you in the gaol until the circuit judge comes to Bacall. When you'll be tried under due process of law.'

'If Will Gershel and his neighbours won't hold still for that?'

'I'll do the best I can to make sure they do, son. But I'm one against many. Giving you advance warning. If any of the homesteaders stop a fatal bullet from your gun and those that are left don't get a noose around your neck . . . in my book, you'll be a murderer. Gunslinger like you shooting down an ordinary working man.'

Polk gazed expectantly at Gold and there was silence between them for several seconds.

'Back in your office, you told me to stay in town. Seemed to me then that you meant it.'

A nod. 'I sure as hell did, son. When my mind was fifty-fifty about believing you or not.'

'Now you're telling me to leave.'

'I can't tell you that, son. Not while there's the matter of more killings, and a rape, to be cleared up.'

He heeled the gelding forward.

Gold held the wooden-butted Peacemaker down at his hip. Squeezed a finger to the trigger and brought his left hand across the front of his body. Fanned the hammer.

Six rapidly-fired bullets thudded into the dead tree. The

gunsmoke drifted away and was neutralised by the warm air of early morning.

Sheriff Floyd Polk looked back over his shoulder and halted his horse to witness the shooting.

'That meant to be a threat, mister?'

'No, sir. Just doing what I came out here for.'

'You're good.'

'I'm getting there.'

'But staying here, I reckon?'

'Found out real young that avoiding trouble was no way to deal with it.'

'You're still young, son. If you get to live much longer, you'll find out the world has no place for people like you.'

Barnaby Gold was holding up the Peacemaker, loading gate thumbed aside, so that the expended shells fell to the ground as he rotated the cylinder.

'Then maybe people like you will allow me to live in a world of my own, sheriff.'

CHAPTER SIXTEEN

THE lawman heeled his gelding into a canter and was soon out of sight on the south trail down into the river valley.

Gold holstered the reloaded Colt, then exploded six more shots from the gun on the swivel rig. Spacing them several seconds apart, but trying for speed as well as accuracy with the mother-of-pearl, eagle-butted gun that had a cutaway trigger.

Then he reloaded the Peacemaker, fixed it back on the gunbelt, and sat down on a fallen tree trunk. Lit a cheroot and watched as the town of Bacall began to go about its daily business now that breakfast was over.

As always, what was running through his mind was not displayed on his clean-cut, evenly tanned, green-eyed, handsome face. He neither frowned nor smiled, scowled or looked pensive. He was just a young man, sombrely dressed, waiting for something to happen. Totally unworried. And utterly confident.

When all the men had left their homes to go up the curved street, and after several mothers had brought their children to one of the houses which obviously served as a school, he rose from the tree and re-entered Bacall.

That he was not welcome there was obvious from the

way many of the men had looked at him. And it was equally apparent, from glances the women directed at him, that it was not usual for them to accompany their children the short way to their lessons – his presence in town was the reason for the break in routine.

Halfway up the street, he entered the gunsmith's store to restock the loops in his belt with .45 calibre shells for the Peacemakers. The owner was nervously anxious to be of service and blatantly relieved when his customer left.

Next, Barnaby Gold crossed the broad street to go into a clothing store. The man behind the counter was the short, pot-bellied, white-bearded one who last night had demanded Jake and Chester be buried outside the town limits of Bacall. His attitude and expression were far less servile than those of the gunsmith.

'You want somethin', mister?'

'When I rode into town last night, there was a caped ulster coat in your window, sir. Black.'

The prospect of doing cash business improved the man's temperament. 'Took it out just this mornin'. Make it a point of changin' the window display once a week.'

'It's not been sold then?'

He came out from behind his counter and went to the far side of the store. Where some items of clothing were heaped on the table. He sorted through the heap.

'Reckon it'll be just your size, young feller.'

He found it and Barnaby Gold shed his frock coat to try on the one that interested him. It was of the same dark colour as the old one, reaching to the same length – three inches below his knees. With deeply plunging lapels below which were six plain, brass buttons. The cape attached to it had a collar with a strip of velvet trimming around it.

'I'm right about the size, ain't I?' the storekeeper said eagerly as he directed his customer to a full-length mirror.

Then cleared his throat. 'But them revolvers give us a problem. Wouldn't you say?'

'Sure.'

Gold released the holster ties from his thigh and unbuckled the gunbelt. Buttoned the coat.

'I got the belt for it here, too,' the eager storekeeper called as he went back to the table.

'No need, sir.'

Gold fastened the gunbelt back around his waist, outside the coat. Studied his reflection in the mirror and clicked his tongue against the roof of his mouth.

'Needs somethin' else, wouldn't you say, young feller?'

Gold saw the man's image in the mirror. He was holding out a long, black silk scarf.

'Appreciate it, sir.'

Gold took the scarf, looped it around his neck beneath the collar of the cape and tied it loosely between the lapels of the coat.

'Looks good.'

'It's fine, sir. You sell boots here?'

'Sure do. Come look.'

He kept them under the counter and after getting Gold's size began to bring several pairs up into view. A highly shined pair, low heeled and reaching just to the level of the coat hem was chosen. Jet black, and slightly decorated with stitching down the outsides. With sufficient room for Gold to tuck his pants legs down inside them.

'How much do I owe?'

'What about a new shirt, young feller? A necktie, maybe? Some underwear? Hose? Hat?'

'Nothing else.'

'Sure thing.' He began to write figures on a pad, then totalled them. Checked the addition and showed his arithmetic to Gold. Who paid for his purchases and headed for the door.

'Appreciate your help, sir.'

'Pleasure, young feller. Pity about you wearin' them guns over such a fine tailored coat, though.'

'Sure is.'

He went out, closing the door on the bearded old man who was shaking his head disconsolately.

Fred Street's livery stable was on the other side of the street from the clothing store. The man was still suffering from the effects of last night's drinking as he curried the horse of one of the dead Channon guns. Gold paid him what he owed for a night's stabling and feed for the black gelding, then saddled the animal and led him outside.

Every business in Bacall was now open and the low-key activity of the town was briefly interrupted by the sight of the newly-garbed Barnaby Gold leading his saddled horse toward the Riverside Hotel.

People in the bank, the mortician on the threshold of his funeral parlour, the preacher talking to two women out front of his church, the expressman helping two others unload crates from a flatbed wagon in front of the stage depot and even a group of Chinese in the laundry all temporarily stopped what they were doing to glance at the passing stranger in Bacall. Then the chores and the talk recommenced.

Across from the hotel where Gold hitched the gelding to the rail, work on the new building was in full swing. One of those involved was a signwriter. On a board painted white he was starting to letter in red: BACALL SCH.

'Town's goin' to have a proper schoolhouse,' Arnie Dalton said as he turned from nailing planks across the frame of the shattered window. 'Bacall is goin' to be some place some day.'

'Charge me for the cost of a new pane, repairs of the balcony, when you figure out how much I owe for room, board and the whore, Mr Dalton.'

'That's not necessary. Fred Street's havin' the horses and saddles of them men you shot. Payin' for the repairs. Givin' the balance to the town toward the cost of the school.'

'Okay.'

'You want your bill? You leaving?'

Gold halted at the batwings. 'Soon as Sheriff Polk gets back.'

'Me and Fran and Annie, we told Floyd how it happened. That you had to defend yourself.'

'He told me.'

'If he has to go all the way down the valley to the Engel place, be some time before he gets back to town.'

'Get breakfast?'

'I'll have Fran see to it.'

'In my room?'

'Sure.'

'Appreciate it.'

There was nothing in Arnie Dalton's demeanour to suggest he was aware of what had happened between his guest and his wife during the night.

Gold went into the freshly-cleaned and deserted saloon and up the stairway. The bathtub, pails, towels and cake of soap were gone from his room. So was Anne Kruger. The bed was neatly made with fresh covers. The Murcott, his saddlebags and the three pieces of the shovel were on the bureau. The window was open and he took the chair over to it and sat down. Ten minutes later called: 'Come in,' when knuckles rapped on the door.

'I didn't want to, but I always do it. It would've looked odd if I didn't bring up the food.'

'It doesn't bother me, Mrs Dalton.'

She brought the tray to him and he took it from her without getting up from the chair. She looked drained and tense from the emotional strain of coming up to his room.

'Thank you.'

'For what?' He started to eat the breakfast of ham, eggs and beans.

'Not allowing me to sully myself as Arnie's wife. He's a fine man. A good man.'

'Deserves better than you, lady.'

'Everyone makes mistakes.' She had obviously struggled to control her impulse to anger at his terse insult.

'You cook well, Mrs Dalton.'

'Dear God, don't you have an ounce of human feeling in you, man? Can't you at least say you understand I wasn't my normal self when I shamed myself in the night?'

Barnaby Gold clicked his tongue against the roof of his mouth. 'Lady, there's a good chance that pretty soon a bunch of men are going to ride into this town from the south. With a lynch rope they aim to put around my neck. That being so, I don't have the inclination to give a shit that you're not getting your share of – '

'I hope they come!' she hissed through teeth clenched in a sneer. 'And I hope they put that noose around your rotten neck! So I can have the pleasure of watching you die, you cold-hearted bastard!'

'Sure, Mrs Dalton. I can understand that. A woman like you has to get her pleasure wherever she can.'

She vented a strangled cry, whirled and ran out of the room. Slammed the door in the same forceful manner as had Anne Kruger on previous occasions.

Barnaby Gold finished his breakfast in peace. Then took his saddlebags and the shovel downstairs and out of the saloon. Stowed them in their accustomed places and returned to his room. He saw neither the Daltons nor the whore.

He smoked a cheroot halfway down before he heard the thud of many hooves hitting the southern end of the street.

And clicked his tongue against the roof of his mouth.

CHAPTER SEVENTEEN

WILL and Jesse Gershel were riding at the head of the group of men. In back of them was Festus Wolfe and the other homesteaders who had converged on Bent River Crossing to gun down Clinton Davis in mistake for Barnaby Gold.

Fourteen riders in all, dressed in work clothes but armed with revolvers, rifles and shotguns. They galloped under the town marker sign and began to slow their mounts as they rode between the houses at the foot of the sloping street. Then reined them to a halt in the commercial, mid-town area of Bacall. Where merchants and clerks emerged from doorways to gaze through the settling dust of the halt at the grim-faced, unshaven and weary-looking men in the saddle.

'Okay, you people!' Jesse Gershel yelled, taking off his CSA forage cap, running a shirt sleeve across his sweat-beaded brow and replacing the cap. 'We don't want none of you pokin' your noses into our business!'

He glared at the apprehensive townsmen.

'Shut your mouth, boy!' his father growled. And made the same survey to either side of the street: but with no belligerence in his grim-set face. Said: 'You folks need our business, ain't that right?'

There was a long silence as each citizen of Bacall waited for another to speak. Until the gunsmith blurted:

'Ain't no one can deny that.'

'We hear a stranger named Barnaby Gold is here in town?'

'Best you don't mess with him. Folks like you: and him bein' what he is.'

'Advice ain't what we come for!' Will Gershel countered, and the gunsmith backed into his premises. 'You folks know what he done?'

'He killed a couple of gunslingers down to the – '

'I mean to us!' Gershel cut in on the white-bearded, elderly owner of the clothing store. 'He raped the Engel child. And shot her Ma and Pa. Then he gunned down JL Larkin.'

Gasps and cries of shock rippled along either side of the broad, sun-bright street. Will Gershel waited for the noise to subside. Then: 'Where is he?'

'Floyd Polk rode out into the valley after talkin' with the kid,' the clothing storekeeper said.

'Polk can ride to hell and back, for all we care! Yellin' at the top of his voice about due process of law and the rest of it! Won't alter nothin'! Where's Gold?'

Now there was angry aggression on Gershel's fleshy, time-lined and element-darkened face as he swept his narrow-eyed gaze along each side of the street.

'Damnit, you can't ride into this town and . . . '

Again the white-bearded man was cut off in mid-sentence. By Jesse this time.

'Don't tell us what we can't do, old timer!'

Another tense silence.

'We'll search through every damn buildin' here if we have to!' Will Gershel snarled.

'Let's get to it, Will!' Festus Wolfe yelled.

'There's only two places in town rent rooms!' the gunsmith called from within his store, to silence the vocal agreement given to Wolfe. 'And he ain't stayin' at the boardin' house!'

The elder Gershel set the pace for the group. Heeled his horse into an easy walk up the sloping curve. The other homesteaders closed into a tighter group to the sides and behind him. Drew revolvers from holsters and rifles from boots: unhooked shotguns from saddle horns.

Doors were slammed, some of the townsmen shutting themselves in their premises – others waiting until the gun-toting riders had gone by before running in the opposite direction to be with their womenfolk and children.

At the arched entrance of the church, the gaunt-faced preacher implored: 'Let there be no more violence here.'

And was ignored.

'Hey, Pa! That's his horse hitched outside the saloon!'

Jesse's voice rang out above the sound of running feet, as the men working on the new schoolhouse dashed for shelter into the laundry, despite the chattering protests of the Chinese.

With the revolver clutched in his right hand, the Gershel boy unhooked a coil of rope from his saddle horn. One end of this was skilfully formed into a hanging noose. His father used hand gestures to signal the homesteaders into a single line along the centre of the street, horses turned to face the façade of the Riverside Hotel.

For a second after the mounts were still, just the rippling of the creek around the bridge pilings disturbed the silence.

'You Daltons and the whore!' Will Gershel roared. 'And any other innocent folks inside! Come on out here!'

Hammers clicked back and the lever actions of repeater rifles were pumped. Sweat beaded every hard-set face. Here and there, hands trembled. Eyes shifted in sockets, transferring suspicious stares from the batwinged entrance to the windows on both lower and upper floors. Raked the roofline. Gazed at the corners of the building.

'All right! Don't shoot! Me and Fran are comin' out!'

Fear quavered every word Arnie Dalton yelled. Two pairs of footfalls sounded on the floor of the saloon. The batwings were pushed open slowly and the Daltons showed themselves on the threshold, the husband with his arm around the shoulders of his wife. They stepped down off the stoop as the batwings flapped closed at their backs.

'Where's Annie?' a homesteader asked.

'I don't know. Up in her room, I guess. She should have heard you, Mr Gershel.'

'Maybe the sonofabitch is holdin' her hostage, Pa!'

'Can we go?' Fran Dalton rasped fearfully.

'Yeah.'

'Thanks.' Dalton blurted his gratitude, took hold of his wife's elbow and hurried her out across the street: heading for the law office on a course that took them past one end of the line of mounted men.

The woman looked back several times at the façade of the hotel. Waited until she and Arnie were at the doorway of Polk's office before she shrieked: 'The open window on the balcony! That's his room!'

Her husband wrenched her forward and sent her staggering into the law office.

A dozen gun barrels were tracked to the target and the triggers were squeezed. The sound of the fusillade caused several of the horses to rear and back away. One of the homesteaders, cursing his mount, was pitched from the saddle.

The window of Barnaby Gold's room was shattered. Splinters of wood exploded from the frame, the surrounding timber and the balcony rail. Some of these shards showered down on to the black gelding below and the horse, schooled to be calm at the sound of gunfire, was panicked by this rain of debris. He wrenched up his head and the hitch in the reins was loosed. He wheeled away from another hail of wood chips that a second volley of bullets gouged from the hotel façade: then bolted down the curving slope of the street.

Jesse Gershel had been first to fire at the open window: his act spurring other men to blast at the target. But now his father re-established his leadership, not having exploded his Purdey in the barrage.

He leapt from his horse and bellowed: 'I wanna see him hung! Let's go get him if he's still alive!'

He lunged into a run across half the width of the street. Others aped his actions.

'Pa, watch out!'

Jesse was still trying to control his spooked horse. He glimpsed a movement at the corner of the building on the creek side. And as he shrieked the warning, he triggered a shot through the billowing dust and drifting gunsmoke.

Other homesteaders reacted instinctively. Whirled and exploded shots at the same target. Still others turned in the same direction, tracking their guns. But did not fire them. Were older and slower in their moves. Had time to see the target more clearly. Shouted counterwarnings to that of Jesse against the crackle of the gunfire.

'No!'

'Don't!'

'It's not –'

'It's –'

But Anne Kruger was already going down on to her knees. Blood blossoming on the white fabric of her dress. At the belly, chest and both shoulders.

The shooting had been curtailed, but horses were still stamping and scraping at the ground, snorting and snickering. These sounds covered the crack of the whore's knees impacting with the hard-packed dirt of the street. Then she sprawled out prone.

'We friggin' killed her!' a man blurted in dread. And hurled his Winchester to the street, as if it were the rifle and not he who was tainted.

'Oh, my God,' Will Gershel rasped.

Started toward the bullet-riddled woman. But pulled up short when she turned her head and raised it. To gaze at Gershel and the other men with eyes that were filled with dismay rather than pain.

'I just come to tell you . . . he ain't in the hotel. He run off down the hill . . . out back. Into the trees . . . toward the river. Why you do this to . . . ?'

The agony of the multiple bullet wounds hit her and the words were curtailed. So that she could vent a keening scream. Then she died. The scream became the death-rattle in her throat and her head banged back against the dirt.

'Pa, I thought it was him!'

Jesse's shrilly-voiced excuse ended perhaps three seconds of utter silence during which even the horses were calm in the presence of tragic death. And caused all eyes to shift their awe-filled stares from the corpse to the frightened boy.

For a longer period of silence, Will Gershel seemed poised to lunge at his son. Needing this action to release the unbearable seething rage that reached to his every nerve ending.

'Pa, don't!' Jesse croaked. 'It was an honest mistake.'

'That's right, Will,' the man who had thrown down his rifle added.

The elder Gershel squeezed his eyes tight closed. Snapped them open and snarled: 'She told us what we needed to know before she died, you men. And she didn't oughta die for nothin'. Go get him.'

The men left their horses to do Gershel's bidding.

'Alive unless he wants it the other way.'

The homesteaders moved into two groups to go around the hotel at either side.

'Not you, Jesse!'

Will Gershel stood still at the front of the building. And as he snapped this final order, his son froze in the act of turning. To stare at his father, fearful that the threat of a violent assault had not yet finished.

'Why, Pa?'

The elder man held his silence until the footfalls of his friends and neighbours had faded from earshot on the timbered slope out back of the hotel. Then: 'You're just too damn eager to kill him before we can put that rope around his neck.'

'You noticed that, too, Mr Gershel,' Barnaby Gold said.

CHAPTER EIGHTEEN

HE stood at the glassless window with the bullet-holed surround. The Murcott angled down at the Gershels from his hip, left hand fisted around the twin barrels and right index finger to a trigger.

The father turned and tilted just his head to look up at the black-clad figure. The son swung from the waist and started to bring up his revolver.

'Don't be a fool!'

The father shot out a hand and fisted it around the barrel of the revolver.

'What have I got to lose, Jesse?' Gold asked evenly.

The father dropped his Purdey to the street. The son groaned and surrendered his revolver. The father dropped his, too.

From across the street and along the curving side of it that offered a view of the façade of the Riverside Hotel, the citizens of Bacall watched and waited: as tense as the two men who stared up at the twin muzzles of the shotgun and the implacable face of the man who aimed it.

'Pa?' Jesse said, and seemed on the verge of weeping.

'How'd you get the whore to do what she done for you, boy?' Will asked.

'I haven't seen her since I left her in my bed first thing this morning, Mr Gershel.'

'You expect me to believe that?'

'No. But you're in a position where you have to listen.'

'They'll be back soon, Pa.'

'Shut your mouth and listen, Jesse.'

'Appreciate it. Figured it wrong. Thought the last place you'd look for me was where you were told I was staying. What with my horse hitched to the rail in full sight.'

Will Gershel nodded. 'I figured it right, boy. Figured your kind can only get by doin' the unexpected.'

'Was too late to change my plan after the Daltons left and you started to shoot. Had to hit the floor and wait it out until you quit it. What Anne Kruger did was as much a surprise to me as you.'

'Guess she must've liked you real well, boy.'

'Sure.'

'So what now? You've made it so she died for nothin'. Showin' yourself like you have.'

'She did what she wanted. What I'm doing. Because I didn't do what the Engel girl said I did.'

'All I'm doin' is listenin', boy. On account of, like you said, I ain't in any position to do much else with that shotgun aimed at me and Jesse.'

'Other people are listening, too, Mr Gershel. Bacall people who aren't from the river valley and before that from Tennessee. Who don't think that everything you do is right so a stranger has to be wrong.'

'Tell it, boy.'

Barnaby Gold did so. Even-voiced and expressionless. Loud enough for his words to carry partway down the curving street. Just as he had told it to Sheriff Floyd Polk earlier in the day. A witness in his own defence at a weird murder trial held on a sun-bright street. The stand was the bullet-shattered window. Jesse's crazed stare marked him as the prosecution. The listening citizens of Bacall formed the jury. Will Gershel, as impassive as Gold, was the prejudiced judge. The horses were disinterested spectators.

He told of his early morning arrival at the Engel place. Of seeing a man ride away. Of finding the corpses of Virgil and Mary-Ann Engel. Of Joanne's admission of guilt and involvement of Jesse. Of her threat and how she carried it out at the Gershel homestead. Of Jesse's story that he stayed out all night because he was sick from liquor. Of Joanne's taunts when he was a prisoner in the Gershel's parlour. Of JL Larkin's evidence that Jesse was fine when he rode past his place. Of Anne Kruger's account of Jesse not getting drunk – instead, just enraged by envy of Clinton Davis going upstairs with her. Of how he, Gold, had remained in town instead of resorting to guilty flight. Of how Jesse was the first to start shooting at Davis in front of the Wolfe homestead, at the hotel window in the wake of Fran Dalton's shout and at Anne Kruger when he thought she was Gold.

'And I guess he was the one,' Barnaby Gold concluded, 'who talked you people into holding off from coming to town. When the two gunslingers rode up the valley and told you they were looking for me.'

Will Gershel shook his head. 'Somethin' else you figured wrong, boy. That was my idea. Seemed like the sensible thing to do. Them bein' the same kind you are. And outnumberin' you two to one. Why risk our lives if others was prepared to take care of you?'

'And why have my death on your consciences, along with the way you killed Clinton Davis? When you couldn't be sure I'm guilty?'

'You're guilty, boy. Only reason you stayed around here was to show how big you are. But you ain't big enough to get out of this. The townspeople heard you spout all that stuff, same as me. Heard you tell what old JL Larkin and the whore is supposed to have said.

Which wasn't much. And they're both dead anyways.'

'Hey, that's right, Pa!' Jesse grinned.

'Shut up, boy!' Will Gershel did not look away from Barnaby Gold at the window. 'So what d'you figure the townspeople are gonna do? When the men come back up out of the timber? And you're gonna have to either start shootin' or give yourself up without a fight. Maybe Jesse and me'll be dead. A few other men. But so will you, boy. Shot dead, or hung for whatever new killin's you do here.'

Gold clicked his tongue against the roof of his mouth. 'Everyone is destined to die some time, Mr Gershel.'

'Your time has come, boy,' a man said from the open doorway of the bullet-ravaged room. 'Now, with a bullet in your back. Or you can hang.'

Gold turned his head slowly. And saw Festus Wolfe standing on the threshold, aiming a Winchester from his shoulder. He had taken off his boots to enter the rear of the hotel and climb the stairs. The same as the other two homesteaders who had moved into the doorway to flank him. They aimed revolvers.

Down on the street out front of the hotel, Jesse Gershel stooped to reach for his discarded hand-gun. His father kicked it clear just before Jesse's fingers were about to close around the butt.

Gold let go of the Murcott and it hit the window-sill and bounced down on to the balcony.

'Now take off the gunbelt,' Wolfe ordered tensely.

'Sure.'

He unbuckled it and let it fall to the floor. All three men in the doorway vented sighs.

'We got him!' Wolfe yelled.

The rest of the homesteaders came out on to the street. Emerging from around both sides of the hotel.

Gold looked out of the window just before strong

hands gripped both his upper arms. Not to survey the grim-faced men and the grinning boy immediately below. Instead, to rake his expressionless green-eyed gaze along the sloping curve.

It was deserted, the widely spaced buildings on either side giving no sign or sound that there was anybody inside them.

'Wasn't nobody heard you who's goin' to help you, boy,' Festus Wolfe growled, moving out of the room ahead of Gold and the two men who held him prisoner.

'Like a lady said awhile ago, Mr Wolfe, everyone makes mistakes.'

'Too late for you to learn from this one.'

CHAPTER NINETEEN

HIGH tension augmented the heat of the blazing sun to bead every face with sweat as preparations for the lynching of Barnaby Gold were made.

Will Gershel had taken the rope from his son and broken from the group of his friends and neighbours. To ignore the footbridge and wade across the creek ford. Heading for a tree on the other side of the trail from where a mound of fresh dug earth marked a two-man grave.

Some of the homesteaders gathered the reins of the horses and began hitching them to the rail outside the hotel.

Festus Wolfe continued to aim his rifle at Gold while the two other men who had made him a prisoner in the room held his upper arms. And Jesse Gershel took a length of twine from a pants pocket to bind the captive's wrists behind his back.

Except for the area out front of the Riverside Hotel, the entire length of the street remained deserted.

Gold gazed directly ahead, ignoring the sweating men close to him to look at Will Gershel. Watched him as he tossed the noosed end of the rope toward a stout branch some fifteen feet from the ground. At the third attempt he succeeded in looping the lynch rope over the branch. Kept his back to the activity in front of the hotel when he yelled: 'All of you bring him over here! Bring a horse, too!'

'Yeah, Pa!'

Jesse hurried away from Gold to unhitch the reins of a horse from the rail. This as the men holding Gold's arms urged him forward.

The other men shuffled to obey Will Gershel's command.

From the law office came a strange sound. Like laughter. But also like sobbing. The sound of the venting of hysteria. Silenced by the crack of flesh against flesh.

The booted feet of men and the hooves of a horse splashed in the slow-moving, shallow water of the creek.

Drops of water and beads of sweat dripped from the men to the dusty surface of the trail on the other side of the creek.

'Get him up on the horse.'

Still Gershel avoided looking at Gold's implacable face. By stepping up behind him, to knock off his hat and place the noose around his neck as he rasped the order.

Jesse giggled as the prisoner was awkwardly raised and settled in the saddle: his shiny-booted feet not in the stirrups.

'Shut up, boy!' He cleared his throat and spat at the ground. 'There's a man about to die here!'

He held out the loose end of the rope.

'What you want, Will?'

'I want every one of you men to have a hand on this. When I set the horse to runnin'.'

'He's your son, Will,' one of the homesteaders complained, taking off his hat to wipe a shirt-sleeved arm across his forehead.

'The Engels were friends and neighbours to all of us, Clyde.'

There were grunts of reluctant agreement. Then Clyde was second only to Jesse in taking a grip on the lynch rope.

Will Gershel now moved forward, to stand alongside the horse and look up at Barnaby Gold: who sat erect in the saddle, gazing across the rippling creek and down the curving, deserted street. The older man on the ground was outwardly more tense than the one in the saddle.

'Anythin' you wanna say, boy?'

Hoofbeats hit the southern end of the street, the horse and rider hidden by the intervening buildings on the curve. Voices shouted, indistinct over the distance.

'Just Goddamnit to hell I never got to Europe.'

'That all?'

'Bye-bye.'

A shot rang out from the direction of the galloping horses. And a whole chorus of voices were raised.

'Hit the friggin' horse, Pa!' Jesse's words were shrill, almost like those of a woman.

'You just gotta have a death wish, boy,' Will Gershel said in strained tones.

Sheriff Floyd Polk raced his horse around the curve and into view of the lynch mob and its intended victim. Fired his revolver into the air a second time. He continued to yell at the top of his voice, but the words were lost under a cacophony of sound. The hoofbeats of his horse. The running footfalls of Bacall's citizenry as they wrenched open their doors and spilled on to the street. And the din of a wagon and team being driven hard up the hill behind the lawman.

'What the hell?' the man at the side of the horse growled.

'We do things our way, Pa!' Jesse roared. And lunged forward. To bring down his splayed hand on the rump of the horse.

'No, boy!' Festus Wolfe cried.

The horse snorted and leapt from a standstill: his head going up to jerk clear of Will Gershel's hand reaching for the bridle.

Polk reined his mount to a skidding, turning halt. And was thrown from the saddle out front of the hotel. This as a flatbed wagon came hurtling around the curve of the street in a cloud of dust. At the same moment as the animal spooked by Jesse raced across the ford.

Barnaby Gold was still in the saddle, the noose around his neck: the rope trailing behind horse and rider – every man with a hand on it having let go at the moment Jesse made his frantic move.

The black-clad man with his wrists lashed together at his back fought to stay astride the bolting horse: knees pressed to the saddle fenders while his feet sought the stirrups.

The animal came up out of the creek just as Polk regained his feet – reached as Gershel had done to try to grip the bridle. But the horse veered suddenly to the side, frightened more by the sight and the sounds of the braking, slewing wagon than by the attempted capture.

Barnaby Gold was pitched in the opposite direction. Could do no more than tuck his chin down on to his chest and bring his knees up to his belly. He hit the street with his right shoulder and hip. The breath rushed out of his lungs and a sea of boiling pain washed over him. He thought he screamed his agony aloud, but could not be sure. For sounds were being vented from too many other throats.

He rolled over twice and then came to a halt. On that side of his body that felt on fire with the effects of the fall.

He had instinctively closed his eyes. Now he opened them and orientated himself.

He was up against the water trough, facing out across the street. First saw Sheriff Floyd Polk who still had his gun drawn, but hanging down at his side. The lawman was staring toward the creek. Barnaby Gold, his vision blurred by spontaneous tears of pain, looked in that direction. Saw the homesteaders coming across the ford. Will Gershel in the lead, having to half-drag Jesse by the wrist. The boy was directing a string of babbling words at his father, who showed no sign of hearing.

Down the street, in front of a half-circle of Bacall citizens stretched from one side to the other, was the stalled wagon with a sweat-lathered team in the traces. Something close to a dozen women had climbed down from it. Gold recognised Martha Gershel and Gertrude Wolfe. The young woman he had seen take her child into the house when the stranger rode by. And Joanne Engel held between two women he had never seen before.

'Mr Gershel, you can thank your –'

The Gershel father and son went right on by the lawman, followed by the other men from the river valley. And the tense and suddenly enraged Polk curtailed what he was saying. Began to whirl, but caught a glimpse of Anne Kruger's body sprawled face down at the corner of the hotel. He cursed and went toward the dead whore.

Gritting his teeth against the pain it caused, Barnaby Gold forced himself up into a sitting posture against the water trough.

'Explain yourself, woman!' Will Gershel thundered.

'Tell him, girl!' his wife responded woodenly.

The group of men had halted some ten feet in front of the gathering of women. All the homesteaders were equally grim-faced, with the exception of Joanne Engel and Jesse Gershel. She looked proudly defiant: he expressed deep-seated dread.

'Go to hell, all of you!'

Martha swung toward the girl trying to act a woman. And backhanded her hard across the cheek.

'Tell him! Tell everyone here!'

Polk had crouched to look at the waxen face of the dead whore. Now he came to the water trough, and helped Gold to his feet. Took out a penknife from a pants pocket, opened it and cut through the wrist binding.

'Appreciate it, sheriff.'

'You tell it, woman,' Gershel demanded of his wife.

'All right, Will!' she snarled. But then moderated her tone. 'I had my doubts, right from the time the stranger brought the girl to our place. Ain't none of us livin' in the valley don't know about the womanly airs this child puts on. But I kept tellin' myself it was her ways give encouragement to the stranger to have his way with her.'

'All right, Ma, but that don't mean I had nothin' to do with –'

'Shut your mouth, boy!' his father rasped, still holding him by the wrist. Tightly enough to make Jesse wince with the pain of the grip.

'But then I kept thinkin' about Jesse bein' gone from home all night for the first time ever, Will. And about him and the girl been walkin' out together for so long. Him a man with man's needs and her a child with ideas ahead of her years.'

'All that thinkin' don't mean not a damn thing, woman!'

'You didn't come home last night, Will.'

'We waited at Clyde's place. Ready to come into town, see if two gunslingers had taken care of Gold for us.'

'Must've hidden themselves real well when I rode by,' Polk growled sourly.

'I couldn't sleep from worryin', Will. Stood it as long as I could, then I went down to Virgil's and Mary-Ann's.'

'They're dead, ain't they, Martha?' Festus Wolfe asked fearfully.

'They're dead, right enough. Sure as the girl been taken by a man. But it wasn't the stranger responsible for any of it.'

Like almost all the women from the wagon, she wore a waist apron over her dress. Now she delved a hand into its front pocket. And drew out something that glinted in the bright morning sunlight. A half-dollar sized silver medallion with a silver chain threaded through an eye on one edge.

Martha Gershel held the chain at either end, so that the medallion swung slightly at its centre.

'See what it is, Will?'

Her husband made a wet sound deep in his throat. 'The lucky token we give Jesse on his fifteenth birthday, Martha.' He sounded drained to the brink of exhaustion.

'It don't mean nothin', Pa!' Jesse vented a sob at the end of this.

'Where'd you find it, woman?'

'In the girl's bed. Chain broken, Will. In the bed where Jesse and she – '

'Shit, it's true!' Joanne Engel blurted out after remaining so arrogantly defiant throughout the telling of Martha Gershel's story. And thus claimed the shocked attention of the audience. 'Jesse did it to me! And I didn't try to stop him! My Ma, she was wed at my age! So was lots of you women! Yet me, I was supposed to wait! Well, frig it, I wasn't gonna wait! Jesse come to me and we done it! Now I'm a woman! And he's a man!'

'No, Pa, she's lyin'!'

'Shut up, boy. What about your parents, girl?'

'They was up at Bent River Crossin', visitin' with the

Wolfes. Jesse saw the wagon there so knew they was away. But after we done it, we went to sleep. They come back. Must have seen Jesse's horse in the barn. Crept into the house. Found us in bed. Started yellin' fit to bust a gut.'

She paused, and something close to a smile spread across her freckled features as she looked around at her audience. The women flanking her, the men in front, and the townspeople behind. Enjoying their shocked reactions to her bald telling of what had happened.

'Jesse's gun was on his clothes on the floor by the bed. I grabbed it and shot them. Virgil first. Then Mary-Ann. They fell down, but they weren't dead. Jesse took the gun and finished them off. Then we buried them out at the barn. And Jesse and me done it again.'

Gasps and groans rippled through the arc of townspeople. The women who had already heard the girl's story remained tight-lipped. Their menfolk muttered soft curses and blasphemies.

'She was sleepin' sound as a baby when I got back from the Engel place, Will,' Martha said bitterly. 'I roused her and said we had to come to Bacall. At Bent River Crossin', I showed her the lucky charm and she told me and Gertrude what she just told you people. So we come here quick. The other women joined us on the way. When we met up with Sheriff Polk and told him . . . told him, too, that you menfolk weren't home . . . he come on ahead to get here faster. Try to keep you from doin' what you was to the stranger.'

All eyes now swung their attention to where Barnaby Gold had been standing. But he was no longer at the water trough. Just Polk stood there, coiling up the lynch rope removed from the young man's neck.

It was the man named Clyde who said: 'We're much obliged to you, sheriff.'

Other homesteaders nodded and grunted their agreement with this.

'Then show it by handing the Gershel boy and the Engel girl into my custody,' the lawman answered.

Movement was glimpsed at the shattered upper storey window of the Riverside Hotel. But nobody paid more than passing attention as Barnaby Gold, his gunbelt buckled back around his waist, leaned over the sill to retrieve the Murcott from the balcony.

Because Will Gershel became the centre of concentration when he said: 'That ain't our way, and you know it.'

'Pa, what you gonna do?'

'We're all gonna do it, boy.'

He released his hold on his son, and snatched the revolver from the boy's holster. Backed away from him. The other men also opened up a gap between themselves and the terrified Jesse.

'You women. Push the girl out alongside him. And stand clear.'

'Will, you can't!'

'Gershel, put up the gun!' Polk drew his own six-shooter as he tossed the coiled rope into the water trough.

'I said we're all gonna do it!' Gershel snapped. And cast a glance to either side. Grunted when the other homesteaders pulled revolvers from their holsters.

'She's just a child!' a woman pleaded.

'And he's your own son, Will Gershel!' another added.

Martha gripped Joanne Engel's upper arm and pulled her away from the two who held her. For a moment it seemed as if she was going to protect the girl. But then she pushed her firmly toward where Jesse stood.

'They're both murderers of innocent people. They wanted to be grown-up. Grown-up folks have to face the blame when they done wrong.'

The women opened up a gap behind where the boy and the girl stood.

Joanne began to cry. Every inch a child again. Arms hanging down at her sides and head bowed. Between her sobs she spoke words. About her 'mommy' and 'daddy' and how sorry she was for what she had done.

'Pa, you can't, you can't, you can't!' Jesse wailed.

He whirled around, saw his mother and held out his hands to her.

Barnaby Gold stepped through the batwings as the first shot was fired.

Exploded by the revolver in Will Gershel's hand. To crash a bullet into the back of his son.

'No, Festus!'

'Clyde!'

'John, don't!'

'Phil!'

The shrill pleas of the wives were all but masked by the crackle of guns fired by their husbands.

Jesse and Joanne were down on the street. Screaming for a short time. Then silent. But still moving. Jumping to the dictates of their punished nervous systems. Then jerking at the impact of each new bullet that tore into their flesh. To spurt blood through the gently rising dust.

Then the last gun was emptied of its final shot. And silence had an oppressive physical presence in the hot, bright, morning air.

'Holy Mother of God!' a woman in the half-circle of townspeople gasped.

Gershel looked to the side, his face drained of blood beneath his element-stained skin.

'We'll take our dead home on the wagon, sheriff. And there's an end to it.'

Polk slid his gun into the holster. 'For you people it'll never be ended until you die.'

Gershel shifted the direction of his blank-eyed gaze a little to the left. Said to Gold who stood before the closed batwings: 'We came real close to makin' a bad mistake, son.'

Barnaby Gold, the shotgun canted across the front of his body, a cheroot angled from a side of his mouth, clicked his tongue against the roof of his mouth.

'But keep this in mind,' the homesteader went on. 'You were the rock that dropped into the heap of shit and set it to flyin'.'

'And none of us came out from under it clean,' Polk growled as the bullet-riddle corpses of Jesse Gershel and Joanne Engel were gently lifted and placed on the back of the wagon.

Under a pall of melancholy, the women climbed aboard the wagon and their men unhitched their horses and swung into the saddles. The crowd of townspeople dispersed.

Fred Street came around the curve, leading Gold's black gelding and the bay which had been used for the abortive lynching.

Will Gershel took the bay from the liveryman, who came on up to the hotel with the black gelding.

'Appreciate your trouble.'

'Guess the saloon ain't open?' Street asked, licking his lips.

'It's open,' Arnie Dalton assured as he came across from the law office.

His wife was not with him and from the long, hard look he directed at Barnaby Gold who was swinging astride his horse, the saloon keeper had learned from her some version of what happened during the night.

'I'll need to have Annie's body removed. Then find out how she died.' Polk eyed the mounted man quizzically.

'Bacall's own undertaker can take care of her body, Floyd,' Dalton growled.

'Damn waste of womanhood,' Fred Street muttered as the batwings flapped behind him.

'And the whole town can tell you Gold didn't kill her. There ain't no reason at all for him to stay here.'

'I left twenty dollars on the bureau in my room, Mr Dalton.'

'It's too much. You need some change.'

'To cover what I owe. And pay for the whore's funeral. Bye-bye.'

He clucked to his horse and tugged on the reins to head him across the creek ford.

'And nobody'll be sorry if you never have cause to say hello again, mister!' Dalton called sourly after him. 'Now Annie's dead.'

Barnaby Gold halted his horse, dismounted and retrieved his hat from under the tree at the side of the trail. Swung into the saddle again and struck a match to light the cheroot. 'No chance of that, sir. Bacall isn't between me and Europe anymore.'